RAVEN'S

RESURRECTION

A suspenseful story of inspiration.

YVONNE DeBANDI

This book is a work of fiction. Names, characters, places and incidents are products of the author's imagination or are used fictitiously. Any resemblance to actual events or locales or persons, living or dead, is entirely coincidental.

Learn more about the author at
http://Evie-Marie.com

Before you strike out in anger,

Before you say words that you don't mean,

Before you turn and just walk away,

ask yourself, what would Jesus do?

Special thanks to Jamie Jordan, Terri Helton,

Forrest Fortier, and Gwen DeBandi

for their support and encouragement with this project.

CHAPTER ONE

Maybe it was time. Maybe today was the day. Maybe nine years was enough to hide, to blame herself, to forget.

Raven stood, leaning up against a wall, in a dark corner of a dark little bar about fifteen miles outside of Jackson Hole, Wyoming. Her layered hair hung unusually down her face before flowing down her back, allowing only her eyes, nose, and part of one cheekbone to protrude from behind the long curly curtain. Most people shrugged-off her unusual, abundant and unruly hair as a stylistic choice; but, those that took a closer look would see it was by design.

"Crazy hair suits you," her best friend, Jessie, had said years before. "You know when you put it all together, it's like a Picasso. It's abstract, but it works. I love the red, keep that. In fact, don't hit me; but this look suits you better than anything I've seen on you!" *Jessie always knew how to say just the right thing, although Raven did kind of want to hit her.*

Raven had only been living in Jackson Hole for about six months; but, she already knew everyone in the bar by name. Truthfully, she could probably fill up the entire *Jackson Hole Daily* with "Fun-Filled Facts About Your Neighbors," but they would find it hard to write more than a paragraph about her. They only knew her as Raven, Denny's Goddaughter, a sweetheart that would *'share a smile'* and was *'so easy to talk to,'* or so she had overheard more than once.

Denny's Den was not an establishment found on the local tourist beat or even on any of the maps. While most of Jackson Hole was dedicated to bringing in tourists, this was the place the locals hung out; and, like every other Wednesday night, it was packed.

The room itself was rustic, and felt more like a cozy community cabin than a bar. On the south-side wall, a large fire roared inside a massive multi-colored stone hearth. Small neutral-colored sofas and easy chairs were littered around the open space with your standard round tables covered in red-checked tablecloths. It all added up to the perfect recipe for quaintness.

Raven could see the flames of the fire dance in and out of the occasional smoke ringlets which were ascending from the occupied tables in between. Mesmerized, she watched them drift straight up to the ceiling, where they were summarily sucked into the deluxe air-filtration system. Denny hated smoke, but without even looking Raven knew he would have a stogie in his left hand. It was a Wednesday night tradition.

"Lived in with love," is how Denny had described the Den's ambiance during the official welcome tour. Looking around now, she again reflected that it was quite appropriate. The only thing that had probably changed about the place in Denny's ten years as proprietor, besides the air-purification system and Denny's hair going handsomely gray, was the spot above the fireplace where the buck head and many pointed antlers used to hang. As her eyes rested on that very spot, Raven couldn't help but smile as the video-like memory played out in her head.

"It goes or I do," she had said firmly, initiating a familiar stare-down challenge as Denny considered her request.

Denny knew she didn't have to work there as a trade for room and board. She could easily pay rent and expenses with her computer work. He also knew Raven would be perfectly happy stowing herself away in the tiny cabin located at Bear Crossing CabinLand, seeing no one for weeks. Denny didn't like that idea for both selfish reasons and his concern for Raven. She needed to be with people, good people, and maybe he needed her just as much.

Not willing to take the chance, Denny shook his head and dramatically proceeded to remove the beautiful animal and hideous trophy from its decorative position. With a very formal 180-degree military spin, he proceeded to march out to his truck full of pomp and circumstance. Making sure Raven was watching, he tenderly laid it in the back of his truck and covered the item with respect using one of the many tarps from the bed storage box. Snapping into a sharp military salute, he formally whistled a beautiful rendition of "Taps."

During all the ruckus, Fred, Denny's nephew, came running out of the kitchen with a spatula in his hand, holding it up as if he intended to use it as a weapon. He made it just in time to catch the end of the ceremony. Without a word, he looked from Denny, to the fireplace, to Raven, before lowering the kitchen utensil and rolling his eyes with absolute glee. He returned to his kitchen duties chuckling, thinking about how life in Jackson Hole had never seemed so entertaining.

Marna, the young lady who ran the flower shop about five miles down the road after the turn-off, was having her regular mid-day coffee break at the time of the incident. She had made no attempt to hide that she was enjoying the scene, even winked at Raven in response to the change. Later that very afternoon she paraded in with a beautiful large, hand-woven basket filled with dried flowers and sage to set on the mantel. The basket was almost large enough to cover the obvious space on the wall where the wood was lighter in color, a prominent outline where the beautiful animal had been on display.

Marna was 31, just a handful of years younger than Raven, but she was wise for her age. She had always been *the girl with the plan,* a personal detail she had shared with Raven during their first conversation. The story was filled with both confidence and appreciation for how things worked out, but Raven thought she also saw a twinge of regret in her eyes. While her friends had taken their time settling into their lives, Marna immediately opened her own business and had been working hard ever since.

Raven sensed Marna's longing for adventure, for something more, which made Raven smile at life's questions. While Marna sometimes wondered where she would be now had she taken that trip to Europe with her girlfriends, Raven was wondering where she would be now had she taken Marna's safer, smarter road.

Marna was obviously sweet on Denny, despite the age difference. Anyone watching could sense the connection in the air when they talked; but, the conversations never moved beyond respectful, attentive friendship.

Raven's eyes continued to rest on the mantle with the sage basket as her memories played out, but she knew Marna would be sitting at the corner of the bar. It was the closest seat to Denny's habitual standing post. He stood there every evening with an obvious twinkle in his eye, watching over the crowd like a proud papa. It suited him. It had been no surprise to Raven that the folks around here had adopted Fred's term of endearment for his uncle, "Pops."

Denny just touched people that way, something Raven had witnessed all of her life. One thing you knew for sure when talking to Denny is that he would tell you the truth, no matter what, even when it came to the difficult topics; but, he would do so with genuine sincerity and kindness. He was firm and strict; but, also very loving. Simply put, Denny challenged everyone he met to be the best version of themselves.

An active marine for most of his adult life, at 59, Denny looked like he was still physically able to serve at a moment's notice. His initial tour began shortly after he had become Raven's Godfather; but, he had spent every bit of leave with Raven's family. He even had his own room in their home where Raven would hide out during his absence, counting the hours until his return. Raven was an only child and loved her parents dearly, but they didn't "get her" like Denny did, and Denny was not oblivious to this fact.

Like Raven, he was a 1's and 0's man: yes or no, black and white, what's right is right. Questions that had other people turning in circles for days were quick and easy decisions for him. He loved his childhood best friends, Sean and Lydia, who had married almost as soon as their graduation tassels flipped on their square hats, but he felt a personal emotional responsibility for Raven. In his heart, he knew it was his job to help this child reach for the stars that were rightfully hers. Because of this commitment, it was Denny that got Raven started with both playing music and working on computers.

It started when she was seven. Denny was home for one glorious summer month. He burst open Raven's bedroom door to announce his surprise return, presenting a guitar of her very own. In previous years, she would sit and listen to Denny for hours and still beg for more; but, that summer they played together. He taught her the basic chords, how to strum and fingerpick, along with the importance of taking care of the instrument and treating it with respect. Raven practiced what he shared intensely and was immediately addicted, even having to be reminded to eat. That month was glorious. The memories of her parents as the audience while she sang and played the evenings away with Denny, were some of her most treasured.

Raven's MBA-accomplished parents loved and ado   enny,
but they didn't see eye to eye about Raven in many   While
they "allowed" Denny his month of fun with thei   ter, they
thought of music as a hobby and, sadly, a gre   tion. After
Denny returned to his tour of duty, their ir   hat Raven put

the guitar down and do something more useful with her time became unbearable. Demands that finally resulted in the guitar being taken away altogether.

Denny read Raven's short and matter-of-fact letters repeatedly, until he could almost recite them. He understood his friends' position of wanting to protect their child's future, but if they would just "see" who she really was inside instead of simply "looking" at her as who they wanted her to be, Raven would not suffer this intense disconnection and loneliness.

The next week-long leave had Denny returning home with big bear hugs . . . and a computer. He spent the entire week showing her the computer ropes, focusing a good deal of time on software he had installed for her.

"Well," he whispered that first night, "we aren't really hiding hat you are doing from your parents. They were thrilled about the c... uter training and didn't ask about the music software, so I did ell them. But here is the deal. You divide your time. Half of it to m... nd the other half to those programming tutorials . . . after your h... ork and chores, of course. Deal?"

Denn... 't worried about the slight obfuscation of truth. He knew Raven... follow his instructions to the letter, increasing both her artistic talent and ability to join the work force. Doing it this way, without full disclosure, just saved a long three-hour conversation about their "vision" for Raven. That conversation always ended the same way.

Sean and Lydia would outline their rigid plan and Denny would respond with, "And what about Raven's vision? Raven's talents? Raven's dreams?"

The answer was like a broken-record: "Raven is too young to know anything for herself, or to recognize personal talents or dreams."

Denny still thought about those conversations on occasion, and more often since Raven's arrival. As he watched his Goddaughter standing alone in the dark corner, he desperately wished he could have that argument all over again. He missed his friends terribly. The year Raven entered high school, her parents had perished in a car crash.

CHAPTER TWO

The bar was packed because it was Wednesday, Open Jam night, and still a couple of days before the official winter tourist season began. No doubt the music was going to go all night long; and, somewhere around two o'clock, Jacob, a scruffy looking regular who worked at the auto shop and loved to barbecue, would start giving Denny a hard time.

"How can you have a bar named Denny's that doesn't offer breakfast? I'm telling you Pops, gold mine! I mean, who here isn't hungry?" he would shout out looking for reinforcement.

Of course, once enough noise was made, Mario would run next door to Mario's Marvelous Pies and bring back enough pizza for everyone to eat and take home, the entire time muttering in Italian under his breath. He loved it, but he would never admit it. Rumor has it that he and Jacob were actually devising a breakfast pizza and, of course, a breakfast barbecue pizza. As of this moment, though, that was still a rumor.

Mario, originally a tourist that decided he never wanted to leave, lived in the cabin closest to the restaurant; but, he was never there. If you were looking for Mario, you would find him standing watch over a pizza oven, tossing dough or attending to other restaurant duties. That applied to just about every day of the week, except Wednesday nights. Tonight, like all the regulars, he sat in his *normal* open jam seat. His was next to the fire with his feet on the logs. Every once in a while, he would shift his position to toss in another, keeping the fire perfectly stoked.

"Ain't no sunshine when she's gone" crooned Kevin O'Connell, the town resident blues vocalist, bringing Raven's focus back to the stage lining the east end of *Denny's Den*. Raven guessed the stylishly-dressed young singer was in his early thirties. His voice was pleasing, inviting, and you could tell he sang for the music, not the crowd. Raven appreciated that about Kevin, even though his arrogance off-stage kept her from being a personal fan.

She was, however, a huge fan of the song. It was the perfect choice for the moment, summing up the atmosphere in the room. Three days until the official calendar start of ski season and so far, no snow. That meant that despite the amazing entertainment and drunken revelry, an untouchable heaviness drifted around the room.

Raven may have been new to the area and never before lived in a tourist town, but it wasn't too hard to understand that a slow tourist and ski season meant a tough year ahead for the town residents. Despite that, everyone was doing their best to forget their troubles, a point made obviously clear as the entire room began to sing along with the bluesy classic. It was loud and out of tune, but also sincere and heartfelt. The latter being all that mattered.

Small towns are great, Raven thought, watching the room with hidden marvel. At least they seemed to be great from her viewpoint of standing on the outside looking in. The town had embraced her and accepted her, but Raven had a knack for turning questions into questions. She understood that most people preferred to talk about themselves and had turned personal space and private vagueness into an artform.

She knew, however, that if she accepted Denny's dare tonight, all that would change. She would no longer be watching from the outside, a mystery, an intrigue not worth the trouble of pursuing. The spotlight would once again illuminate, and the shadowy sanctuary in this dark little corner would be gone.

Despite those thoughts, Raven knew it was a losing battle. The real challenge wasn't whether she could ignore her godfather's dare; but, how much longer she could deny the piano's magnetism when every moment since her arrival, it had relentlessly beckoned to her from across the room.

Mulling over her thoughts, she closed her eyes and smiled in appreciation at the ear-candy offered. The musicians were doing the number true justice and this only made her think about the piano even more. Sighing she pulled out a cigarette and immediately heard the familiar flick of a lighter, followed by words spoken in a proper British accent.

"My Lady?"

"Bugger," she said to herself, silently reciting, "Rule no. 3: never offer an opportunity to approach."

Slowly she turned her head and accepted the flame. As her cigarette began to glow she allowed her eyes to wander up, expecting to find a stranger. She didn't recognize the voice, and Raven was good with voices. Since moving to Jackson Hole, however, she had fallen for this trick every time.

"Wally," Raven sighed more than spoke as he handed her a drink and winked, "Stop doing that!"

"Guuurl, you broke your own rules. Never pull out a cigarette without first lightin' yo flame!" he exclaimed in a gruffly, cigarette-choked voice while staring, waiting for her to defend herself.

Others might have been taken aback by his tone and eye contact, but Raven knew it was all an act. She tried her best to stare at him blankly, noticeably failing as her lips lifted into a smile of their own accord. Wally was good people. That was what her gut said the instant they met, but nevertheless she asked Denny just to be sure. His gut was never wrong, at least not in her entire life.

Waiting for the dramatic scene she knew would unfold, she crossed her arms and looked at him through her long curtain of hair in expectation. Seeing the open window, Wally instantly broke into a brilliantly white, beautiful smile, changing his stance to match his newly chosen accent and character, a much younger version of his previous choice. Wally never turned down a spotlight.

"Gurlfriend, saved you from Table 12, an early-bird tourist that wandered in. Pfft. He don't know no better. Can't blame him. Look at you standing up, all over here alone, in black, in those boots and ripped jeans, with that dark red hair over your face. Since he probably hasn't heard the very kindly put 'hands-off' rule you so clearly established to our locals here, I would have thrown him out for NOT noticing your mysterious, sexy self."

Raven couldn't help but laugh. Wally was a very tall black man, well built, with a smile that lit up a room, a twinkle in his eye and a hug that felt like home. His voice was as smooth as butter with a slight southern drawl when he was truly relaxed, but when working he usually used some sort of accent, playing some sort of character. Originally born in Alabama, Wally had been here for *as long as he could remember*. At least, that is what he said when you asked him. Truth be known, Raven had gathered it really hadn't been all that long.

The adventurous tourist probably pegged him as the bouncer. Easy mistake since Wally liked to wander as he worked and well … looked like a bouncer; but, there was no bouncer in this place. No need. These people respected each other and took care of each other on nights like this when alcohol did come into play. No, Wally was the bartender; and frankly, words seemed to fail when trying to describe his unique and impressive drinks.

Late one Saturday, Raven stayed to help sweep the floors and straighten up. She wasn't sure how closing chores actually took twice as long that night, but then again, they did stop numerous times in fits of laughter. And, the sight of this 6'4" black man rolling on the sofa with giggle fits just made things worse.

That night they came up with the *brilliant* advertising angle: ***Wally, the ARTbender and Spirit Specialist.*** It was the first time Denny had heard Raven laugh like that in as long as he could remember. All he could do was sit in his office and listen with tears streaming down his face, probably for a good hour, before finally joining them hands-on so they could get out of there.

Denny thought the *ArtBender* angle was brilliant. He was having signs and cards made, and also asked Raven, the Den's webmaster, to create a whole section devoted to it. Denny had vision like that, as Raven well knew. It was easy to see . . . and well, taste, that Wally's secret drink recipes were like nothing you could find anywhere else. It was a no-brainer for Denny. He grabbed onto the idea quickly and set it into motion. Not to increase the bar business (although that was definitely a check in the pro column), but to see where Wally might take this interesting and original idea.

As a result, on Wednesday nights Raven could count on a new drink recipe unveiling and was never disappointed. Tonight's concoction was the ***Flaming Leotart.*** The unexpected fire demonstration had been truly impressive and the taste indescribably satisfying. It somehow washed over you smoothly, like a second skin, and ended with a kick of delectable tartness.

Despite this obvious talent, Wally would tell you bartending was his day job, like so many other hopeful actors and artists found behind a bar. With Wally, you never knew what accent or speech pattern you would get during conversation; but, if there was a theater production in town you could bet your life that he would be center stage or somewhere in the front row shouting accolades and clapping louder and harder than any other audience member.

Wally winked again and as he started to turn away Raven said, "Hey Wally, if Fred ever does you wrong, you let me know. We will start a conversion intervention and I will steal you away," Raven quipped as she watched the big beautiful man chuckle with grace.

"Oh yeah. I almost forgot," he said pulling a napkin out of his pocket. The branded paper was covered in scribbles that Raven instantly recognized as Denny's hand-writing.

"Pops said to remind you that you have to do your *thang* tonight. . . Dang girl, you standin' in the darkeeeest corner of the room."

Raven grinned as Wally squinted dramatically, waiting for his eyes to adjust, finally turning the napkin in circles to follow the words written around the edges.

"He says he has upped the stakes. You do your *thang* . . . whatever that is . . . and you get to move to that more private cabin you wanted by the lake at the first of the month. You don't, and he is starting a breakfast shift with you in charge."

He paused for effect, leaned a little closer, lowered his voice like a confidante, and raised one eyebrow.

"So, Miss Thang, what's your thang? Breakfast shift, huh? Pretty serious situation to consider for our resident vampire who doesn't sleep until the sun comes up, hmm? Don't think I didn't notice. Why do you think I started wearing these here turtlenecks?" he asked, ending his speech by stretching the neck of his stylish apparel and letting it pop back into place.

Denny and his nephew, Fred, who helped manage the bar and cook, were the only ones who knew the entire truth about Raven's past. Why she was here in Jackson Hole and why she needed a new start. Truthfully, no one but them even knew her last name. Raven wasn't sure if Wally had been 'read in', but with this playful question, she suspected Fred had honored her privacy.

Wally and Fred had been together for three years now, although when Raven asked how long they had been together, everyone in earshot recited in unison, *"as long as he can remember."* Wally was not a time tracker or a dweller. She often heard Wally answer questions with phrases like, "Doesn't really matter what any of us did before here, what are we doing now?" So, he never asked Raven about her life circumstances. He simply welcomed her friendship in any way she was willing to offer it.

Fred and Wally were a most unlikely couple. If she had just met them on the street, Raven would have never guessed in a million years they could be a perfect match, but they were. Wally with his artistic imagination, flamboyance and style; and Fred, who dressed in plaid, only spoke when necessary, stood tall at five feet if he was lucky, and truthfully was in desperate need of a tan. He was much more like the marine side of his Uncle, but Fred seemed to understand Wally, like Denny understood Raven.

Wally and Raven, who shared the same childlike imagination and wonderment when discussing things that could be created or dreamed, became fast friends. Denny and Fred had even commented to each other, that watching Wally and Raven was like watching two only children who suddenly found a lost sibling.

Needless to say, because of the fun atmosphere being created, bar business was up. Denny wasn't surprised. Simply put, Wally was the biggest drama queen and diva of them all . . . and proud of it. He intrigued people just by being who he was, obviously and outwardly different from the rest of the flock. And Raven had always been a magnet. People loved her. Despite the fact that she didn't share personal details about her life, people loved the way Raven made them feel.

Denny couldn't have found a reality show on the planet that would have turned down the shenanigans that were now everyday occurrences. The two of them together were like magic to watch as they shared their smiles and kind nature with anyone that crossed their path. Of course, it didn't hurt that their childlike games and harmless practical jokes seemed to entertain the guests as much as the two-man jokester crew. Denny firmly believed that some people were becoming daily regulars just to see what they would come up with next.

Despite the twinkle in Wally's eyes, the entertaining vampire reference, and his ability to ask questions without expecting an answer, tonight there was a question of concern. It was almost hidden by his acting skills; but, not entirely. That onion layer had been added when Wally had reached to brush the hair out of her eyes one afternoon. They hadn't known each other very long then. Before he could succeed, Raven had grabbed his muscular arm in her strong little hand, purely out of instinct. Stopping him like a mac truck, she said only one word in a voice he didn't recognize, "DON'T."

The next morning it was like nothing had happened. Except now there was that new look in his eye and fairly regular cracks about how Raven could probably beat him up. But, being Wally, he didn't ask for details and frankly didn't care. The only thing he knew was that voice deep down inside, the voice that mattered, the voice that said it was his job to make that girl smile.

Looking past Wally after hearing the message, she found both Denny and Fred smiling and waving at her across the bar. Wally laughed at the overly done scowl on Raven's face and then stopped cold.

"He knows, Fred knows what the *thang* is, doesn't he?"

Looking back and forth between Raven and Fred, Wally wasn't sure who to pressure first. You see, it was okay not to offer information, but if someone else knew something and he didn't, it festered until he could take it no more. His decision, however, was made for him when Denny pointed at the bar and motioned for Wally to get back to work. Denny then turned directly to Raven and raised his hands in question of her decision.

Reluctantly nodding, and thinking only of the promised beautiful little cabin on the lake, Raven mouthed, "Okay, you win. Last. Put me last."

CHAPTER THREE

As the night wore on, the musicians worked through a stylistic smorgasbord of tunes, leaving almost no style untouched. Earlier in the night the younger musicians had shared some wonderful selections and arrangements, new styles and style moshes that had Raven shouting, *"Bravo!"* Cheers that probably couldn't be heard over the ecstatic parents whose accolades outweighed Raven's by several decibels.

At midnight, however, the crowd shifted. Denny had a "curfew" in place and all underage individuals were booted out, all but one, that is. Michael had a special pass.

It was a larger shuffle than normal tonight, with the youngsters exiting and a new flood of late night workers, mostly over the age of thirty, piling in. As the music continued, both the amount of alcohol consumed and level of comradery grew. The heavy burden that had previously hung in the air evaporated, but not for Raven.

Almost immediately after accepting Denny's cabin bribe, Raven started to think too much. It wasn't that she was afraid to get on stage and it wasn't that she was afraid to perform; in fact, she wasn't afraid at all. Her questions concerned the aftermath. She would no longer be the sweet and mysterious stranger that stands in the dark corner, the girl who freely shares a smile, but refuses to dance and always buys her own drinks. No, after tonight, people would want more.

There was also the question of addiction. Once she allowed herself to touch that piano, could she stop the tide that would ultimately follow? Her addiction and love for the piano far outweighed her love for the guitar. It had a powerful draw that even Raven didn't understand. It made her feel strangely complete; like the piano was a true extension of her own body, reading her mind and dancing along with her fingers. Denny had found her thoughts completely logical.

"I'm not surprised. It's an organized numbers thing appealing to the mathematician in you. I expect a concert when I get home," he had responded many, many years before when she had shared her discovery.

But all of those reasons were small, *minuscule*, compared to the real reasons behind her hesitation.

Raven's thoughts were interrupted as Denny yelled her name across the room. "Raaaaveeeeen, we got musicians and they need a lead. You're up."

There is not much you can do to argue when more than eighty surprised and slightly inebriated people are staring at you in expectation, maybe a little bit of shock, but definitely expectation. Immediately commentary began throughout the room.

"Raven, you play piano?"

"Did you know she was a musician?"

"Does she sing?"

"Get up there! Go Raven!"

Denny was nearly beside himself, pleased with his manipulation as he watched the audience weave the web of no return. Raven needed music to survive, to find herself; and, if Denny had to manipulate such a situation, then by God he was on the job.

A quick glance at Wally, found him frantically mixing a drink, so fast it seemed his hands were blurry. Raven couldn't help but giggle internally at his antics, but came to full understanding when he swooped from behind the bar with perfect timing to hand her a drink as she stepped onto the stage.

"From Pops and me. I doctored it up a bit. I don't know what you're doing, since I know you don't like to draw attention to yourself, but go get 'em girl," he whispered smiling, but with no trace of accent.

"Thank you," whispered Raven in return, moving closer to make sure her words were not overheard. "Um, Wally, if I say the word *asparagus* at any time, can you get me out of here no questions asked?"

Without hesitation, Wally's expression changed to one of complete serious intent as he replied, "in the blink of an eye," offering his hand as support on the last step up.

As Raven took her first sip of the drink, she appreciated that Denny had thought of everything, *well almost everything*, Raven realized as she crossed to the piano. She could hear the audience still making comments about their surprise and excitement, when she heard Denny's voice again, "and by the way, you know you have to start with my favorite, right?"

Raven smiled as someone from the audience said, "Pushy, aren't you Pops?"

As the audience continued to give Denny a hard time, Raven nodded respectfully to the other musicians. There was an upright base, a small set of drums with a myriad of percussion options, and

Grandpa Bernie on jug who had been playing all night long. It didn't matter that he had reached the point hours ago where no tone existed. Bernie might have been short on wind, but he was heavy on gumption. He liked to stay right in the middle of the action and had a permanent stage seat on Wednesday nights.

Having listened to the bass player, Randy, for several weeks, she knew he could follow along with no trouble and that the very talented percussionist, Steve, would add his own unique touch. Raven said, "Let's keep it easy and do it in C."

Raven turned back to the beautiful piano that had been calling to her for months and lovingly stroked the keys. *It has been a while, my friend.*

Clearing her throat, Raven adjusted the microphone, "This one goes out to my Godfather, Denny. My roots, my wings, my strength, my family."

Within moments, the crowd became completely quiet. Raven played the introduction, making love to the piano like someone who has been starved for a tender touch, before singing a most mesmerizing rendition of "Wind Beneath my Wings." By the last note, it was over. Raven knew she could not force her soul to live without music any longer. *Let the healing truly begin.*

As the last note faded, the room stood immediately and applauded, possibly more out of surprise than appreciation; but, before it could get too crazy Denny shushed the crowd.

"Now play us one of your songs. How about the one you sent me on my last tour?"

He loved her Gospel stuff, claiming it stayed with him all day long. Locking his gaze, she could see the twinkle in his eyes. He wasn't fooling around and didn't flinch at Raven's stare. It didn't matter. The demands from others around the room were growing stronger and the piano's calls even louder. Raven's hands began moving out of pure instinct. She was born to do this.

"This is dedicated to those that have suffered at the hands of terrorism. It's called *Reaching for the Light.*"

> As I witness, this darkest night.
> I can feel you, trying to show me the light.
> And I'm reaching, oh yes I'm reaching,
> Reaching for the light.
>
> So many faces, so twisted and dark.
> They don't know You, don't know Your heart.
> They bring terror, like it's their right,
> So I stand, in Your love, reaching for the light.
>
> Reaching for Your light,
> Standing in the light.
> Sharing love and being kind,

I will stand and I will fight,
In Your name by reaching for the light.

You give us freedom to make a choice,
And I'm choosing to use my voice,
On earth as it is in Heaven,
That's the world that I want to live in.

In the light I find the hope,
And the strength to forgive.
I will stand and I will fight,
In Your name by reaching for the light.

Reaching for the light,
Standing in the light.
Sharing love and being kind,
I will stand and I will fight,
In Your name by reaching for the light.

Reaching for Your light.

Standing in the light.

On earth as it is in Heaven,
That's the world I want to live in.

At the end of the song, Raven was torn between the peace the song always gave her, jumping off the stage and out of the spotlight before they could ask for another, or complying with the piano's demands to play until she could play no more. Her hesitation gave Denny yet another chance to control the circumstances.

"Encore! Encore! Encore!" he shouted as everyone else joined in as reinforcement. "Now how about we end the night with *All I Need?*"

He couldn't. He didn't. Could she even make it through that song without breaking down? It had been a long time since she had opened *that* door.

Raven wasn't sure how long she sat there with a blank look on her face, lost in another time. She could feel Denny's and Fred's eyes on her, smiling, encouraging, excited. Glancing over at Wally, she found him bouncing back and forth from foot to foot like he was dramatically preparing to run, with a huge smile on his face shouting "Encore" louder than anyone else. Once again, her fingers started of their own accord, despite her emotional hesitation.

> I can't believe that I'm again sitting here,
> Feeling so alone, when I know You are so near,
> Lately I find there's an emptiness within,
> Maybe it'd be easier if I'd just give in.
>
> But then again, every lesson must be learned,
> And when I stray, You guide my safe return.
> Just when I think, there's no more I can bear,
> I turn to You, You are always there.
>
> I will stand strong,
> No matter what may come.
> I won't be down for long,
> Now the battle has begun.

My faith will win, I'll never give in,
Because it's true, it's You.
You're all I need.

In truth, Denny didn't know what would happen and had his own set of fears. The only thing he did know is that different was good and this girl was born to play music. No one was going to stand in the way of that. He couldn't bear the hollow look that haunted her eyes any more. He thought he had lost her once and now that she was here, damned if he was going to watch her live a half-life. Listening to her sing her own lyrics, "I will stand strong," he knew that no matter what happened, this was a step in the right direction.

Sometimes it seems, like the world's closing in on me,
No peace to be found, chaos at my feet.
But with a single prayer, You dry my tears,
And with a gentle hand, You vanquish my fears.

So I can stand strong,
No matter what may come.
I won't be down for long,
Now the battle has begun.
My faith will win, I'll never give in,
Because it's true, it's You.
You're all I need.

And when it seems every hour is getting worse,
And every word I speak, feels like it's a curse,
I turn to You, to set my spirit free.
Yes, I turn to You, because I believe.

If Raven could have heard Denny's thoughts, she probably would have agreed. She was lost, engaged in the music and the message completely, no longer paying any attention to her surroundings. She was home again in her beautiful musical bubble. The words empowered her as she continued, allowing her to offer more to the song with each lyrical line. And then, as the last chorus began, Raven forgot.

> I will stand strong,
> No matter what may come.
> I won't be down for long,
> Now the battle has begun.
> My faith will win, I'll never give in.
> Because it's true, it's You.
> You're all I need.

She forgot the piano was facing the wrong direction. She forgot to guard herself. She relaxed her body, allowed the full feeling of the song to be shared. The emotional performance resulted in Raven lifting her head, something she rarely did these days. And then as the last note was being held, she lifted her eyes to heaven, tilting up just enough for gravity to swoop in and pull her hair back off her face, allowing everyone to see what he had done to her—how the monster had carved into her like she was his property. The gasp in the room was tremendous, but it was Wally dropping a glass that made Raven open her eyes, startled, but oblivious.

After a moment of deafening silence, while Raven was reorienting herself in this plane of existence, a none-the-wiser Bernie stood up from the other end of the stage, shouting and pointing at the window.

"Hey, it's snowing! It's snowing!"

Raven looked and saw the snow was indeed coming down and fast. Looking around the room, she expected to meet eyes of excitement about the snow; but, no one except Bernie was looking out the window. All she saw was concerned and questioning eyes, making her realize her mistake. The women were holding the side of their face and the men that had come to know Raven, however superficially, looked stricken, trying to hide the tears in their eyes.

Not wanting to explain, but also not flinching or hiding, Raven scanned the crowd. She found her little family immobile, as if in shock. This was obviously not one of the scenarios they had played out in their heads when manipulating this performance.

With a reassuring look and smile that all would be well, she then turned and scanned the speechless crowd with the same "It's okay" expression, albeit with little effect.

To the far left, her eyes came to rest on Michael, the young man with the curfew pass. She had been mentoring him for weeks on how to build websites and attach them to social media sites. His face was contorted with disgust, not at Raven, but at the camera in his hand. As she watched, he dropped it on the table and backed away a few steps like he had just discovered it was evil. Slowly he looked up at Raven in horror, shaking his head, apologizing with his eyes.

These actions slowly, at least it felt like a very long time to Raven, led to the realization that Michael had been putting their last lesson to the test. He had been streaming the entire event live onto YouTube and who knows where else. Although she tried with all her might to not let the smile drain away from her face, all she had left to give at that moment was a disbelieving chuckle at how the night had played out.

"Hah," followed by one word whispered into the microphone, "Asparagus."

CHAPTER FOUR

Raven could feel the sun on her face. It was warm and comforting. There was classical music playing in the distance, one of her favorites, Pachelbel's *Canon in D*. It was so simple in its orchestration, so organized in its mathematical design, no surprises beyond the resulting synergistic harmony and beauty. The music filling her ears, combined with the beautiful sunny field of flowers before her, Raven humored herself thinking the scene would be a perfect example of "serenity" in the dictionary. In the distance, there were many animals running and playing: deer on one side, antelope on the other, and a beautiful tabby cat sitting on the fence post playing with a butterfly. It was a magnificent sight that, very simply, made Raven happy. The resulting smile was so strong that her cheeks actually began to hurt.

Her peaceful thoughts were interrupted by the delicious smell of coffee. Slowly, as the scent became stronger, Raven realized she had been dreaming of her "Happy Place," a technique Dr. Langstrom had suggested a few years earlier. The technique had been much more successful since her move to Jackson Hole. Before her arrival here Raven simply avoided sleep all together; only pure exhaustion allowing her a few hours of reprieve before the night terrors began. Despite the difference her relocation and the fresh air had made, Raven generally spent the dark hours working at a computer screen, waiting patiently for the sun to come up. Only then would she grab a few hours of needed rest; but, not last night.

Still gaining her bearings and refusing to open her eyes, Raven began to reflect upon the events of the night before. Wally, true to his word, had gotten her out of the building quickly. Denny, stricken with remorse, sprinted for his truck while Fred distracted the crowd with a free drink and a grand toast to celebrate the start of a successful ski season. As far as the regulars were concerned, it was the snow that mattered, not the date on some calendar.

With one last look to the crowd before exiting through the back door into the storage and stock loading area, she found a bewildered Michael sitting deflated in a chair. Raven hated that the young boy felt so terrible and understood his position clearly: their lessons had not yet covered how to *remove* videos once they were broadcast. If he had successfully employed the full techniques discussed during their lesson, it would be a few hours task to track it all down and remove the contents.

Humph. Life's little twists.

Not allowing her thoughts to borrow trouble, Raven had convinced herself it was no big deal. In 48 hours, this little fifteen-minutes-of-fame window would be closed; and, she could quietly go back to watching the world from her corner.

The desire for coffee was growing and voices in the distance began to prompt the true beginning of the day. Hiding here certainly wouldn't do any good.

Wait, where was here?

She vaguely remembered kissing Denny on the cheek and putting a finger over his lips to keep him from talking on the drive home. She needed to think and certainly didn't want to rehash the evening's events. The last thing she remembered was putting her head on Denny's shoulder as he navigated the truck towards the cabins at Bear Crossing.

Opening one eye very slightly, Raven found herself on a couch in a room she didn't recognize. Opening both eyes completely found Wally sitting in an easy chair on the other side of a rustic, thick coffee table situated in the middle of the most amazing room. Obviously in a log cabin, there was a red rock fireplace with a roaring fire. All the furnishings looked as if they were hand made from the same trees as the walls. On the far side, there was a counter bar with an opening hidden by closed louvre doors. Raven guessed they opened into the kitchen where the coffee and owners of the muffled voices dwelled.

Beginning to sit up, Raven could feel that Wally's eyes had never left her face while she surveyed the room and, as her brain began to catch up with her wakened state, she instinctively moved to cover her hair over her face.

"DON'T," Wally said, just as forcefully as she had spouted months before in the only awkward moment ever experienced between them. Frozen by his words, Raven stared, not sure what to do or say.

"You are beautiful, Raven. And when you are in your home, with your family, you have no need to hide. And in case you think it makes a difference, I have been staring at you for four hours. There is no part of your face that is not memorized. The only thing that bothered me at any moment was the drool about an hour ago; and, maybe the crazy grin just before you woke up," he emphasized with sincere comedic levity before changing his tone again.

"Now that, the story behind *that*," Wally said, circling his finger while pointing at the carving on her face, "I'm sure that story is as ugly as it comes, but that does not define you. Tell me, don't tell me, I don't care; but don't EVER hide from me again. Deal?"

Speechless, all Raven could do was nod, never losing eye contact with the amazing person in front of her. Their comfortable silence was interrupted by raised voices, drifting in from behind the louvered doors.

"Michael, it is not your fault. If anything, it is my fault. How did I get the piano wrong? I set her up. I forced her into this and I got it wrong. It's my fault," Denny said with sad resignation in his voice.

Without hesitation, Raven planted her feet on the floor and marched towards the conversation she could not let continue. So determined to end the negative words and self-inflicted condemnation, she pushed open the swinging door with too much force causing it to quickly swing back and hit her squarely in the face. Stumbling into the kitchen laughing uncontrollably, she caught the occupants completely by surprise; but succeeded in her goal with the comedic entrance and clumsy curtsy.

As the contagious laughter subsided, she crossed to the coffee and began to pour herself a cup of the liquid gold she knew would warm her from the inside out. Not a word was spoken, but she could feel their eyes on her back. Taking a sip and staring out the kitchen window at the snow-covered ground and the beautiful ornate flakes that continued to fall, Raven finally broke the silence with a quiet but firm statement.

"It is not either of your faults. Something like this was bound to happen. The person to truly blame, thankfully, is not here and enjoying a long stay at Shimmering Heights Cemetery. So, let's not dwell on it anymore."

"Miss Raven, you don't understand. I'm so sorry. I know how you like your privacy. I just really loved what you were doing. I... I... I thought I could surprise you. I didn't know. I didn't know. I'm so sorry," said Michael, the tone of his voice matching the tears in his eyes.

"Michael, it's okay," Raven reassured him, still staring out at the silvery white blanket covering the ground outside. "I'm proud of you for putting what you are learning to work! So today, since you obviously aren't in school," she briefly admonished with light-hearted sarcasm, "we will spend a couple of hours before my shift begins to remove the content, that's all. Easy. No damage done."

She could see Denny out of the corner of her eye, shaking his head, but still not saying a word. "No, Miss Raven, it's more than that," Michael beseeched from behind.

Shaking her head, Raven again refused to make the situation more worrisome than it needed to be, "It can't be that bad. It's not like it went viral or anything, right?"

Turning around from the window, Raven saw that Wally, who had joined her quest for coffee during the laughing fit, was now handing Fred a steaming cup. Fred, who had appeared from somewhere unknown to Raven, was leaning into the kitchen from the living room through the now-open louvered doors. Smiling and nodding good morning to the man she had met at her parents' funeral and had called "family" ever since, she saw the answer revealed in his eyes. Fred never did have a poker face.

"No!" Raven exclaimed, disbelieving, "It was three songs. Okay, maybe it had a surprise ending, not really viral worthy. Not like a basket of kittens on catnip or anything, right? Come on, there is nothing to worry about . . . unless," she said, stopping mid-sentence to look at Denny.

Without speaking a word and obviously still beating himself up, he turned to grab the laptop from behind and silently placed it on the table. He then pulled out a chair and invited her to sit down.

Raven wasn't sure she even wanted to know. Ignorance was bliss, right? Maybe if she just ignored it, it would all go away and she could continue her quiet little life here. She felt Denny's hand on the small of her back, leading her to the chair. As she lowered herself to sit, he relieved her hand of the coffee cup that had somehow grown too heavy for her wrist.

Michael adopted the chair on her left and began clicking away at the keyboard.

"I watched it all night," he began, his nervous words flowing much faster than usual, "taking down what I could, but I couldn't figure out how to stop it from this one particular service, IWatch. It's that new one you showed me that records the feed and immediately broadcasts it to the international video directories? I figured you could help me today because customer service was no assistance, but then about 7:00 a.m., this happened, and the whole thing blew up with thousands and thousands of hits."

With a final tap on the Enter button he slowly turned the laptop back to Raven's full view, avoiding her eyes; but, she could feel the questions burning. She didn't have to see the screen. She had already guessed what was there. Someone had recognized her.

CHAPTER FIVE

Resigning herself to face the inevitable, Raven turned her focus to the screen to see three pictures side by side. One of her unexpected facial exposé from the night before, one of a young girl in a black feathered costume, and one of another girl dressed in a similar manner. Underneath was a caption that simply stated, "Look at the eyes. Have we found the original Ravyn?"

The cryptic headline included a story underneath from Musicmagic21, an avid music blogger and head of the "Kissed" fan club, according to his bio. He shared the history of the all-female group that rocked the world in costume, debuting so many years ago and continuing to tour to this very day.

It shared how the band started out as a single-show school project, a tribute parody of the famous rock band *Kiss*; and, much like their mentor, *Kissed* turned into an overnight sensation. While they sported costumes like the mentoring rock band, with all females dressed as sexy animals, their performances were not parodies at all, but original music showcases.

The article opened the door to Raven's memories, thoughts she had avoided for so many years. Not included in print was the fact that Raven had started her musical career while also finishing college, a stipulation Denny had demanded in memory of Raven's parents. It's what they would have wanted. Raven would graduate, no question about it.

Raven had never argued with Denny about staying at the University. She loved learning, although some of her bandmates would have ditched school without a second thought. Despite the pressure, Raven kept her word. Even when the secret dual life requirements seemed impossible to meet, she always found a way and was thankful that when not in costume, she could avoid the spotlight.

Two years later Raven graduated with honors in both music and computer science, leaving the very next day on a year-long worldwide tour. That schedule repeated itself for many years to come until . . . well, until her life fell apart; but, of course, the article didn't mention that.

The article did mention her bandmates and their bios, which made her remember a time when anything seemed possible: the laughter, the musical kinship, the long rides on the bus where so many songs were written. Those were good times. So many nights ended with laughter echoing throughout the moving tube-like structure; but, that was before. . . before they chose stardom over anything else that was important.

Raven had warned them. She had asked for help, and they did nothing. In fact, in some ways, they had even encouraged their old friend's behavior, saying that Raven could do *"much worse than Richard."* They didn't understand why Raven was complaining about the extra attention or special treatment she was getting, and certainly didn't seem to care that it made her uncomfortable. Richard was only *"looking out for her, after all,"* a repeated scolding that echoed over and over as her concerns reached deaf ears.

Richard had gone to school with them; he was a psychology major who also took courses in music business management. The girls had met him one day in the music food court and, as the opportunities opened up, he seemed to naturally fit in as the business manager. It just sort of happened.

Truth be told, he was quite good at scheduling shows and managing promotion. He took care of everything, all the little details. Raven had actually considered him one of her dearest friends and often marveled at his skills. He made their life on tour so easy, college too. How many times had he pulled strings in order to make things work out? And the stories of road life she heard from others didn't seem to match their experience in the slightest. Knowing then, what she knew now, Raven would have traded the royal tour for the rocky roach motel path in a heartbeat.

Shaking away her whirling memories and ignoring the expectation hanging in the room, Raven sipped her coffee and reviewed the article feed further. She knew it was inevitable that she would see his name, the *savior that made them successful*. The truth wouldn't be printed, she knew that, but her curiosity on this day wanted to know the spin.

She actually had no idea what the record label had done to explain or cover up the circumstances because she had never allowed herself to read newspapers or discuss the topic with anyone beyond her therapist. The door to her past had been closed and sealed shut. There was nothing there but a hollow void, nothing she cared to keep.

Her three college friends solidified that decision as they stood over her hospital bed, their faces showing no emotion at all. They informed Raven that the label had given them an option. Their choices were to either jump on the planned tour with a new manager and a new Ravyn, or lose the contract.

Raven, unable to speak at the time, didn't need words to reflect her thoughts in her one open eye, but her *so-called* friends didn't respond in the slightest. Not sharing Raven's sense of loyalty, their mind was made up and that was it. The fifteen people that knew the truth signed confidentiality agreements. Raven received a settlement to never reveal her association with the band, and life went on.

Raven's suspicions were confirmed a couple of paragraphs down, where Richard was reported as the *hero manager* who lost his life in a fire. The description held a hint of bravado and, at the same time, you could tell the author wasn't buying the entire released story. Maybe the cover up wasn't that solid after all.

The history lesson concluded with the author asking questions about the Ravyn character. He stated how the band had lost its dazzle after the manager had perished and the public had chalked it up to the loss of Richard, "but," Musicmagic21 reflected, "it has always been public knowledge that 'Kissed' was started by Ravyn as a school project. Look at the eyes, people. Maybe there is more to this story."

The side-by-side header pictures at the start of the article clearly showed the original Ravyn was the Raven currently sitting at the round wooden table. Subsequent pictures and screenshots captured from the previous night's performance made it even more obvious. One picture caption even posted the question as to why the currently touring band was **never again** seen out of costume and why Python had taken over singing most of the leads.

Sighing, Raven sipped the end of her coffee as she read, "Raven, if you are the original Ravyn, I have been a big fan since day one and would be honored to help you tell your story."

Deciding she had had enough, she opted to bypass the section that started comparing vocal and piano skills and snapped the laptop shut. She looked up at her worried companions with a small reckless laugh before speaking some unexpected words.

"Well, let the games begin!"

And almost before the words were out of her mouth, somewhere in the distance, Raven's cell phone began to ring.

CHAPTER SIX

"If you all could see the look on your faces right now," said Raven while crossing her eyes at Wally, all remaining tension in the room dissipating with his surprised outburst of laughter.

"What? Here I was all worried that they were going to focus on my face," she quipped. "And no, I'm not going to get that," she said about her incessantly ringing cell phone.

"Is it true, Miss Raven? Is that you?" Michael blurted out in a whisper, unable to help himself.

Raven opened her mouth to respond the memorized line provided by the record label, but was relieved she didn't have to lie. At that moment, there was a vivacious knock at the back door, drawing Raven's attention to the entry way at the end of the spacious kitchen. Marna was peeking in, prompting a chorus of "come in" and "door's open." Seeing her struggle with the doorknob had everyone jumping to assist, but Michael's quick movements had the rest settling back in their comfortable positions within seconds.

"Thank you, Michael," Marna beamed at him as she strolled in like a ray of sunshine. In her arms was a huge gourmet gift basket filled with fruits, coffee, muffins, snacks, and many other hidden items.

"Good morning! I come bringing a healthy breakfast and other goodies!" she said as Michael moved the laptop to the counter and she placed the appetizing basket on the table. "Help yourself! Raven, the banana nut muffins you like are in there somewhere and don't forget to read the card," prompted Marna rather nonchalantly as Denny helped her with her coat.

"The card?" Raven asked in a puzzled voice as Marna pointed to the little ornate-covered gift card covered in purple lilacs, her favorite flower. It read: *Welcome to your new home. Love, your family, the entire Bear Crossing Crew.*

"This is the cabin? I really get to live here? Oh, my goodness. It's beautiful! Thank you so much! Well, what are you waiting for? Give me a tour. Give me a tour! But take a napkin. Don't you dare get crumbs on my floor," said Raven, winking playfully at Fred and giving Denny a huge bear hug to say thanks.

Raven had actually never seen the inside of the cabin. Since her arrival she had been staying in one of the small weekly rentals, which suited her just fine, until she made the discovery. Generally, when she took her walks, she just circled around the main loop, but this day a little overgrown path had caught her attention. Upon following it, she found this hidden cabin further down the trail, sitting right on the edge of the lake. If real estate was really all about location, location, location, to Raven this plot of land was like the pot of gold at the end of a rainbow. It was perfect.

She had asked Denny about it, who immediately demanded her not to return; claiming it was being treated for termites with some very serious chemicals and he would let her know if it was structurally sound when the treatment was complete. Pulling out of the hug she looked at Denny squarely with new understanding,

"This place never had termites, did it?"

"No! And we let the path overgrow on purpose!" Wally burst out with excitement as if the secret had been welling at the tip of his tongue just waiting for the right moment. "Ooooo he was so worried you wouldn't buy that story and go exploring! Come on, come on, wait until you see!" he beckoned to Denny to begin the tour.

Without further ado, Denny motioned around the kitchen, inviting her to look at the beautiful countertops and the convenient and functional kitchen design with just the right amount of cabinets and counter space. There was also a spacious refrigerator sporting a smaller-than-average freezer. Raven laughed as Denny pointed out this feature.

"We knew you needed more space for your fresh vegetables and that the only thing you keep in your freezer is ice cream," gallantly opening the doors to show that it was already stocked full of her favorites.

"Oh, my goodness!" Raven exclaimed, overwhelmed by the thoughtfulness behind all the little details.

Upon re-entering the living room, Wally, of course, ceremoniously holding open the swinging door so that Raven wouldn't harm herself, Fred headed to the far side of the room. Raven hadn't even noticed that section earlier, but as Fred pulled open the drapes hiding the large glass doors, she spotted a cozy little patio with seats around a fire pit looking directly out upon the lake. It was breathtaking. They all stood in comfortable silence, taking in nature's masterpiece.

"There's more!" exclaimed an impatient Wally, still looking like a child on Christmas morning. "Can we show her now?"

This question was responded to in favorable chorus, Denny now beaming, so proud that Raven was able to address the day with such a good attitude. That very morning had him reflecting on the dunking game of life, and a journey that continued to pitch hard balls in her direction. Yet through it all, she still cared more about putting a smile on others' faces. This very nature was confirmed with Raven's next statement.

"I hope there is more. I mean, at least a bedroom and bathroom!" Raven teased as Wally started skipping down the hall begging her to follow. She complied, skipping just as he had with Michael joining in the fun too. The others watched the *children* with amusement, completely entertained.

As Wally passed the first door he said, "bathroom, you can look at that later," and a few more doors, "hall closet, spare bedroom, master bed and bath, study or storage," each one followed by the tag line, although slightly higher in pitch as Wally got more and more excited, "you can look at that later."

And then he stopped and said, "But THIS door. THIS door you must explore." As the others gathered behind, making their way up the hallway Wally demanded, "Drumroll please! Pops, you do the honors. This was your idea. Heck, I didn't even know about this part until this morning."

That statement gave Raven an idea of what might be behind door number five, or was it six? As Denny swung open the door, she could see the beautiful hardwood floor and the wall just behind that was covered in . . . was that soundproof foam?

"Close your eyes, Raven," requested Denny, as he led her into the room with everyone quickly shuffling through the door, not wanting to miss any part of the unveiling. After taking a couple of steps at Denny's direction and turning to her right, Denny took his hands off her shoulders and said, "Open your eyes."

Raven gasped. In front of her, first and foremost, sat a white baby grand piano. Behind that, on the left wall hung several guitars, wooden flutes, a violin, a French horn, and a variety of percussion instruments. To the right side she saw a professional sound booth with her old favorite mixing console sitting right on top. Behind that was a large window of glass. Upon closer inspection, Raven could see that it was an isolation room for recording, currently home to a sweet-looking drum set.

"I don't know what to say. Thank you! I'm overwhelmed. This is amazing. How can I ever repay you?" asked Raven with full earnest, running her hand across the piano. Beyond the emotional debt she could probably never match, this room alone must have cost a pretty penny. Not to mention the specific changes she had already seen, obviously installed or designed for her comfort.

"You don't owe us anything. It's true," stated Denny when she questioned him again. "Sure, we chipped in our time, love, and labor, but you paid for all of this," said Denny quietly, knowing that Raven would never be able to accept charity and definitely not charity of this size.

Raven could have stopped the question there and maybe she should have. It could have been a trust from her parents' life insurance policy or maybe he had gotten a settlement those many years ago too, or it could be something from the "undiscussed." If she had let it go, everyone else would have too. Denny's eyes suggested she wait until later, but Raven was past caring. She was tired of hiding. The people in this room were family and she wanted to know now.

"Tell me, please," Raven asked, completely overtaken by curiosity.

After a slight hesitation, Denny gave in to the one person he would always protect, but could never deny.

"They are from your royalties, Raven. I know you told me you didn't want them and weren't going to fight. But, I couldn't let it go. I fought them, not only for your song royalties, but the entire concept, and won. Merchandise, the whole bit. I mean, if they even sell a *Kissed* pez dispenser, you still get a piece. A small piece, but a piece."

Denny's voice trembled just a bit. He had done what he thought was right and would do it all over again; but, he still had concerns about her response. Despite the beautiful room, it was her past catching up to her present.

"How? When?" responded a flabbergasted Raven.

"You were in physical therapy and staying with Jessie at the time, not even walking yet when we started," he explained. This statement made eyebrows raise around the room, but no one posed the obvious question.

"I paid Jessie with a large portion, just like you would have wanted me to," which had Raven nodding in agreement.

"Jessie and I decided to put the rest away in a trust until you were ready. You didn't want to talk about it. Frankly, we thought you got a really raw deal and had been fighting long enough. So, we fought for you. I hope you aren't mad at us," said the one man in the world that could never make Raven angry.

"Mad?! What an amazing day! Not only was it confirmed that I have the most amazing family here in Jackson Hole, but my Godfather fought the big corporations and won! We need to celebrate," Raven stated with glee before striking a charge pose and directing, "To the coffee and muffins . . . and the Bailey's hidden in the back of the basket!"

Raven's motivation for shuffling everyone out of the room so quickly was that she wanted her first date with the piano to be in private, and knew she needed to vacate the room quickly in order for that to happen. Even as she shut the door behind her, she could feel the piano calling to her.

The crew began making their way back to the kitchen with Raven peeking in the other doors on her way, making exclamations over every observation. They ended up, finally, in the kitchen just as they had started with the addition of muffins and Marna, who was sitting at the table on Raven's right, opposite Michael. They settled into fresh cups of coffee and jovial conversation about everything and nothing, each taking turns sharing their favorite part of the house and favorite renovation story.

A short time later there was a slight lull in the conversation, each person moving towards getting on with their day. But before everyone could disband, Raven couldn't resist. She turned to the young man on her left, who had already surmised from the mornings events that that the article exposing her identity was indeed the truth.

"So, Michael, what was your question again?"

As if on cue, Raven's cell phone began to ring, making Wally forcefully set his coffee down on the table and huff out of the kitchen in the direction of the noise. No doubt he was on a mission to find the source and silence it.

CHAPTER SEVEN

Raven spent the remainder of the week shuffling belongings to her new cabin, setting up her office, and sneaking time to play the piano, all the while keeping up with her responsibilities at the bar. As expected, lunch service was busy that week. Most of the town had either witnessed or heard about the event and their curiosity had not been quelled. She could feel and see them leaning forward and twisting their head trying to catch a glimpse under her cascading curls, wanting to see if it really looked like they remembered or as their neighbor's brother's aunt had described.

The whispers went on for about two weeks, if that, and Raven believed she owed yet another thank you to Dr. Langstrom; for he had repeated one very important statement to Raven, a life-altering statement that turned her perspective around right on a dime. And it was so simple. How anyone could overlook it seemed ridiculous, and yet people did all the time.

"YOU and YOU alone teach people how to treat you. If you act like a victim, they will treat you like a victim."

So, instead of shying away from the whispers, Raven would smile at them with understanding eyes and sometimes even wink. Her attitude was, *it is what it is.* She tried to protect everyone from knowing the truth and it didn't work. Oh well. So, the cycle of shock and awe passed to concern and then to curiosity, then to "what a good sport," and finally to the comedic relief that was presented four Open Jam Wednesdays later.

Someone had passed out little temporary Raven tattoos, which presented the actual bird with her name. The name was the truly curious part. The "V" in the middle was transformed into a heart with an arrow shot through it. It was significant to Raven because the very first *Kissed* album cover had featured the four characters with signatures. This tattoo resembled that signature in every way except the spelling. On the album, of course, the spelling reflected the costumed character, *Ravyn*.

When Raven first arrived that Wednesday night, having returned to her cabin for a date with her white baby grand when food service ended, Wally was waiting on pins and needles to be the first to show her. She came running in and headed straight for the bar, afraid she was going to miss the latest drink unveiling. Wally and Fred had their backs to her like they were conspiring something and were startled by her winded blurt.

"Did I miss it?" she asked as her friends slowly turned to face her with huge grins on their faces.

Seeing the tattoo on both Wally and Fred's left cheek in front of her . . . one challenged to stand out among the dark rich color and the other jumping out at you like it was 3D, made Raven laugh in surprise.

"What in the heck is that?!!"

Wally changing his stance to Raven's favorite character she lovingly had named "Otis," the same character he had used the night all this had started with that napkin challenge.

"Guuurl, don't you be thinking you are going to be the only one around this fine town sporting artwork on your face. Didn't you hear? It's all the fashion rage now. See for yourself. Turn around."

Laughing at Fred's expression of excitement, she turned to see many of the same people that had witnessed her first performance there, all beaming at her with tattoos on their faces. The comedic motivation to make light of the entire situation filled Raven with glee. Denny was also grinning from ear to ear, standing in the middle of the crowd, the only one with the tattoo on the right side of his face.

"I see you are still having trouble with your left and right, Denny," Raven jibed which of course resulted in boisterous laughter around the room, causing him to turn a handsome shade of pink.

The evening progressed with much fun and laughter as different combinations of musicians performed as desired, or when called in to help complete the instrumentation needed. Raven joined in too, having become a regular jammer since that fateful night.

Tonight's *ArtBender* special had been, no surprise, called the *Branding Iron*. While Raven had no idea of the recipe, she could certainly identify the apricot brandy peeking through.

Brandy always made Raven melancholy. Perhaps that is why somewhere near the end of the night she sat at the bar, perfectly content, watching Wally and Fred flirt, Denny and Marna pretending not to flirt, and Michael running around with his camera getting close-ups of the musicians and crowd shots. Some of the audience members were actively posing for action shots and others were shying away from the camera; both scenarios were quite amusing to watch. And for the first time in as long as she could remember, Raven felt like she had a home.

The years following the "incident" had been spent with Jessie, Raven's best friend. Because Denny was still occupied with his military career, Raven was put into the social service system when her parents died. Her foster parents had been kind, but Raven practically lived at Jessie's all throughout high school. So anywhere with Jessie felt like home; but, not like this.

As Raven recovered, she knew she wouldn't live there forever. The home she shared with Jessie was home only because of Jessie's presence. This place was different. She might just be able to plant her roots here, in Jackson Hole, in that little cabin on the lake.

Jessie was a nurse at a big hospital in Memphis, but immediately made arrangements to take a leave of absence. For four years she had worked as a full-time house nurse for Raven. There was a slew of doctors and seemingly endless hours of physical therapy as her broken body slowly mended, but through it all, there stood Jessie.

The best part about Jessie's disposition was that she refused to take any slack from Raven and gave her a good kicking whenever needed to push her towards recovery. In the beginning, there were some pretty dark days. Raven wondered what she was fighting for, thinking of only the betrayal, uttering hopeless phrases like, "Why bother, I don't really have anything to go back to." This had Jessie kicking the emotional support into high gear.

Despite the tears, pain, and emotional healing needed, Jessie never allowed Raven to feel sorry for herself. Raven was extremely grateful of that fact. There were times when she would have given up all together had Jessie not been there with unflinching belief that she could recover 100%. Jessie also constantly reminded her that His plan would be revealed as He wished, but the plan was definitely not for her to give up, to keep her faith.

Of course, had it not been for Jessie, Raven might not have been given the chance to recover at all. Jessie was the one who had contacted Denny with concern so many years ago, questioning Raven's whereabouts.

By that time, Denny had retired from the military and had just purchased Denny's Den and the land where Bear Crossing now stands. He reassured Jessie that Raven's schedule was always changing and maybe she had gotten it mixed up. But, upon hearing that Raven had intended to surprise him with a visit first, one that never transpired, and Raven's voicemail was full with no answer, Denny immediately left Fred in charge and jumped on a plane to Memphis.

Once Denny arrived, Jessie shared all of her concerns. It started when Raven didn't show up for their, "I'm going on a tour" stop-over. It was a ritual. One only they knew about. Raven never put it on her official calendar anymore because of a private luncheon that had been interrupted by paparazzi. Richard and the label, of course, claimed they had nothing to do with it; but, from that point on they communicated in code via email, just like they used to do with handwritten notes in school as teens.

At the end of her previous tour, she had emailed Jessie with her flight arrival date and time, via code of course. The message said that she would be out of touch (due to expected sketchy cell reception) at a private studio somewhere in the mountains writing songs. Then a surprise stop-over in Jackson Hole before arriving in Memphis.

Three months had transpired between the writing of that email and the scheduled date of the surreptitious rendezvous.

CHAPTER EIGHT

Taking another sip of her *Branding Iron* and smiling at Wally's wink from the end of the bar, Raven sighed with a mixture of contentedness, melancholy, and curiosity of what was to come. Realistically, how long could she ignore her cell phone before people started showing up on her doorstep?

Sighing again and immersed in her own thoughts, Raven rested her elbow on the bar, supporting her head, chin in the palm of her hand. Feeling the uneven skin and markings beneath her fingertips, Raven wondered when the inevitable truth explosion would occur; and, when it did, how much truth should be told? Was there a purpose for sharing such darkness or should it be left there, in the past, not given any power to spread by not giving it the power of words?

The entire incident seemed like a dream now to Raven. If she did not have such an obvious physical reminder reflected by the mirror every day, she might have been able to convince herself that it never really occurred. She still had no idea how the situation had gotten so out of control. It all happened so fast, yet had started so small, so gradually.

Of course, the best manipulators leave you believing you asked them to do something because you got an idea, when the entire time the manipulator's goal was to get you to ask for that very thing. For Raven, it ended up meaning control of her calendar, her contacts, providing car escorts, etc. For Richard, it meant he knew where Raven was every single minute of every single day.

Had Raven not turned everything over to Richard so willingly, perhaps he would not have been able to orchestrate the multiple-month window with no one noticing she was gone. But that was not the case; Raven had relied on Richard for everything. All through college, all through the tours, he took care of every single detail.

Raven, being the leader of the band and having her fingers in all band decisions, her schedule, and therefore her time with Richard, was much more extensive than the other members. Despite her growing concerns over the years, it was just how things worked. All attempts to reorganize this arrangement had failed. It was out of her control.

At the end of the last tour with *Kissed,* Raven mentioned going to surprise Denny and doing some songwriting, maybe even helping him out in his new bar. Immediately Richard chimed in saying he had already booked her a private studio, like she had asked. He would be driving her there immediately upon landing.

Raven didn't remember making such a request and really wanted to catch up with Denny to celebrate this new phase of his life, but Richard pulled another effective manipulator trick. He stood on his soap box and gave an exposé about how much trouble he went through to make her every wish come true, how changing her plans was completely taking him for granted. It was too much to bear and always easier to give in. Raven agreed to go, figuring a couple of weeks and she would be on her way to Jackson Hole, and of course to her secret stop-over in Memphis. This being the same plan she had emailed to Jessie.

* * *

For the first two hours after Denny's arrival in Memphis, they compared notes and made phone calls, trying to find a starting point of Raven's activities once the tour ended. The answer was always the same, "Find Richard and you will find Raven."

"You know I never liked that guy," said Jessie. "I'm really getting worried, Denny. The way he looked at Raven always creeped me out, and he was screening my calls like I was some pesky news reporter. I don't think I got to actually talk to her in person a single time last year. Thank God for email," she said, shuffling papers and contact information with exasperation.

Jessie's statement made Denny realize that he didn't even know Richard. He had always seemed unavailable and never around after their first initial handshake. In hindsight, Denny mulled that he should have recognized that as a warning sign.

Another two hours of attempts to contact Richard were completely unsuccessful and, with a scared look on his face, Denny picked up the phone one last time.

"I think it's time to call the police."

At the very moment Denny was making his missing person's report, Raven was laying on a cold, stone floor, covered in her own blood, reciting the Lord's Prayer and asking for the strength to attempt one more plan.

CHAPTER NINE

The trip to the mountains with Richard had started innocently enough. There was standard conversation and comments about how the tour had gone, possible improvements for the next tour's show, and a little bit of gossip about who shagged who over the last year. Richard always liked to go there and Raven always did her best to steer the conversation in another direction. As long as what other people did didn't affect her life, she didn't want to be involved.

"Dang, you were right about service up here. I don't have any bars at all." said Raven. "Will make it difficult to send songs for review, don't you think?"

"I'll take care of it, Raven," reassured Richard.

"You'll take care of it? How are you going to do that? Can you transform yourself into a tower or something?" said an irritated Raven.

She had noticed that any time she asked a question he didn't want to answer, that was his canned response. What if she didn't want him to *take care of it*? What if she wanted good reception so she could take care of it herself? She hated the way he could make her feel like a queen one moment and completely helpless the next.

Richard didn't respond and sat in silence until he said, "You know, Argus over at the label had an interesting idea the other day."

Raven searched her mind for Argus. Argus. Argus. Argus. Oh yeah, Argus. "The smooth new marketing executive that wants to 'Shake Things Up'?"

"Yeah, that's him. I actually really liked his idea, but you won't like it," said Richard with coolness.

"So, what was it?" queried Raven impatiently when it became obvious he wasn't going to continue.

"I'll tell you in a minute. Sing this song to me. I love the way you sing this song," said Richard breathlessly as he adjusted the radio volume to suit his request.

Not being able to resist the invitation, and preferring to sing over talking anyway, Raven complied. As the love song drifted off her lips, she noted a change in Richard's expression and before she had a chance to blurt out a topic of conversation, Richard asked, "How about dinner tonight before you get started?"

Trying to steer the conversation in the right direction, Raven joked, "I will definitely need dinner before getting started. I'm starving!"

"So, it's settled then, it's a date," said Richard smugly like he had finally outwitted the coyote.

"Weeeeell, it's dinner and we will be having it together since it is just the two of us, but not a date," she stated as lightly as she could, turning to look out the window and wishing someone else was in the car with them.

"Raven, why won't you give me a chance? One real date? After all I have done for you, is one date really asking too much?" demanded Richard.

"Richard, we have talked about this. Beyond the fact that working together and dating is not an option, you don't want to date me. We bicker all the time. You want to date *Ravyn*, this fantasy version you have created in your head that sings every song personally to you. C'mon, you know that's true. It wouldn't work. You know I love you and you are like family to me, and family is forever. Isn't that better? Besides, when have you ever seen me date?" demanded Raven seemingly all in one breath.

"What about Keifur?" questioned Richard in a suggestive manner.

"What about Keifur?" spit Raven quickly.

"You have a date with him before we meet for the next tour. I heard you. I know you like him," accused Richard.

"Richard, we have a meeting about the new lighting rig. And whether I like him or not isn't really any of your business," clarified Raven.

"It damn well is my business. Everything you do is my business. Why don't you date? Don't you want to have kids? Why don't you date?" said Richard again, trying to keep his earlier coolness, but beginning to falter and repeat himself when no stronger, more pointed inquiry could be found.

Ignoring the initial control statements but noting the internal radar flag, Raven sighed and asked, "You want me to tell you another reason? Again? Fine. As you already know full well, there are many reasons. First, all of my girlfriends in school were nuts over boys. They changed the way they dressed, the way they talked, they would do anything to not be alone. Sometimes after they dated a boy for a long enough time, I didn't even recognize them. I didn't ever want to be that way, and besides, I was never alone. I had Denny. Look at him. He never dated or got married and he is perfectly happy."

"And, I certainly don't want to declare myself to a man for the rest of my life just to have children!" continued Raven. "If or when the right dance partner comes along, I'll know, and then I will consider it. Until then, I'm happy just the way I am. Why can't you accept that?"

"Well, how do you know if you don't try?" Richard asked as he reached and grabbed her hand tightly where it rested on the front seat. "You know we are great together. I'm always there for you. I would do anything for you," manipulated Richard, having regained his full composure.

"Richard, I appreciate you. I am grateful for you. I love you like a brother. I don't mean to be insensitive, but you are making me uncomfortable," whispered Raven sincerely, but with an air of defiance as she wrenched her hand from his grip. Trying to lighten the mood and move onto another subject, Raven asked, "So what's the big Argus idea?"

"He thinks the other girls are holding you back. He thinks you ought to consider going solo. The two of us as a team, without the baggage, would be unstoppable in his opinion; and, I have to say, he's not wrong," suggested Richard bluntly.

"What?! Uh, no. You know I would never betray the girls like that. We have been through far too much, plus I don't agree. The four of us together are much better than me without them. If those are the types of ideas he is coming up with, I may have to get him removed from our team," threatened Raven with irritation.

"Oh, c'mon Raven! You write the songs, you teach the girls their parts, and you design the sets and produce the show. Without the confines of *Kissed*, who knows what you could do! You are so amazing, and you don't even know it," insisted Richard with his best reassuring tone. "Let me help you be the person you are supposed to become. I see it; you don't. I'm the only one you can truly trust."

When Raven didn't respond he asked softly, "Will you think about it? Will you please think about all of it?"

"Yes," said Raven, and she was thinking about all of it. She was thinking about how she felt like a prisoner. And while all the actions were done in the essence of "helping her" or "believing in her," she was a prisoner nonetheless. It didn't matter that the captor thought she was amazing, although it did make Raven feel bitchy to yell at a guy who had just finished saying those very words. And never would she throw away her friends for a bigger, better deal. What was he thinking?

Raven couldn't honestly say that being with Richard had never crossed her mind. Before *Kissed* was even the inkling of an idea, they had run into each other at a few musical events in school and shared a dance; but, when the third dance turned into the let me "pull you closer" stage and hold your body "like I own you," she had had the *friend talk* with him. It was the same talk they had about every nine weeks. Raven used to wonder if she watched the moon, would the cycles somehow match up.

They arrived at their location just before dusk and Raven had to admit the place was amazing. It was a very old house, designed to look like a castle. To say the least, it was huge.

Exiting from the entry way and drawing room there were many hallways speckled with large wooden doors, magnificent tapestries hanging on the walls, fine wood furniture, marble statues, and ornate gas lights hanging from the ceilings on sturdy chains. The decorating scheme was mostly neutral, dark browns and grays, with many portraits and paintings scattered in an organized manner around the immense walls offering a vast array of colors. There would be no need to soundproof this place, Raven thought. The walls were far too thick for noise to escape.

After showering and sorting her things, Richard called her down for dinner. Upon her arrival in the cozy family room, which she found by following his voice, a romantic candlelit table setting came into view.

"Richard," Raven said softly, but firmly, "this is so not cool."

"Stop it. We've known each other forever. Come sit with me here and have a glass of wine, your favorite, a late-harvest Meritage. Tell me, does Kiefer know your favorite wine?" he asked, patting the seat next to him before pouring her a glass.

Ignoring his poke, Raven surveyed the room. There really were no other seats nearby. The little table was off to the side and she wanted to avoid the intimacy it suggested at all costs. The antique desk in the corner and the little sitting station by the window didn't seem to offer any valid retreat either. There was only the small burgundy velvet sofa with fine gold trim where Richard was sitting, the odd-shaped coffee table that looked like it was made from an actual slab of stone, and the plush rug in front of the fireplace. She could sit on the rug, but he would no doubt come and join her. With veiled eyes and stiff posture, she sat down as requested.

After several moments of silence, Richard leaned back, put his right arm around her shoulder, and started kissing her neck.

"Richard, STOP IT!"

In response Richard whispered in her ear softly, eerily, "Raven, you will always be mine. I'm done waiting. Argus wants us to get married. I told him we would be married on our return. There is a huge surprise ceremony planned to kick off your solo tour. Consider this trip an early honeymoon, my love."

As Richard spoke, he was deliberate; and, his right hand around her shoulder was forceful. Returning his gaze to the fire, he slowly swirled his left wrist along with the wine. As the wine repeated its circular motion, the liquid legs clung to the sides of the glass, reminding Raven of her own. Trying to stand once again found her firmly lodged by Richard's grip.

"Richard, let me go!"

Turning his head to match her eyes he said, "Never," and then his expression went vacant, uncaring. "Don't worry, you will come around. You have four months to come to terms with the new arrangements. Take as long as you like," he smirked as he removed his firm hold and settled back on the sofa.

Processing. Processing. Processing. *Oh my God!*

Looking around the room, Raven realized the windows were closed with heavy wooden shutters that looked quite similar to the heavy hallway doors. Wait, had she seen a single open window since she arrived?

Standing instinctively and backing away to put as much distance between them as fast as she could, Raven turned and began to make her way through the house. Her cursory search revealed no accessible windows, no phone, and the front door, the only one she could find thus far, was locked up like a fortress . . . and of course, no cell signal.

An hour later, she resigned herself to the fact that Richard had been planning this for a long time. She was his prisoner, and standing in the doorway looking at the back of his head, listening to him hum Endless Love, Raven knew she was in real danger.

CHAPTER TEN

The first week was filled with bickering as Raven shunned his advances. They had been friends a long time and Raven worked every angle she could to bring the man before her back to reality. And of course, when he wasn't looking over her shoulder, she was searching the house for some means of escape and then, one day, something miraculous happened. Her cell phone beeped.

Running in the direction of her handbag, she pulled the phone out just in time to see Richard barreling through the door and grabbing the phone out of her hand. With dismay, all Raven saw was the top text message sitting on the screen. It was from Keifur.

Raven had never seen Richard this angry. And while Raven must have been confused, she swore she saw him crush her cell phone with his bare hands. In three strides, he had covered the distance between them and savagely began kissing her.

Richard, having a good two feet in height and at least a hundred pounds more than her, the struggle was intense. Kicking and screaming she scratched him down the face, resulting in him backhanding her across the room. She landed with her head on the corner of the dark cherry wood antique bedroom dresser, the force causing her to lose consciousness.

Upon opening her eyes, the room was pitch black and she was tied, naked, to the bedframe, a thick rope knotted around each appendage. Trying not to panic, but losing the battle, she tried in vain to set herself free. She struggled until she could struggle no more, the rope twisting and burning into her wrists and ankles, and that was when she saw him standing over her watching, slowly undressing, before climbing on top of her. Raven lost her virginity that night as Richard raped her repeatedly, demanding the entire time, "Say you are mine. Say you are mine," until she passed out again.

Raven had no idea how many days had passed and considered later that she should have started a stick calendar somewhere, but that wouldn't have been practical anyway. She couldn't see the sun so she didn't really know when it was day or night, and he was always moving her to a different room. She was always naked and had seen none of her belongings since the night her cell phone was destroyed.

It was a blur of hours for Raven. In addition to the sexual and emotional abuse, Richard used tactics like withholding food and drink, chaining her legs to the bed post as he dunked her head in water, the entire time asking for those two complicated words, "I'm yours." She gave in on occasion, not being able to take any more.

She needed to buy some time. She knew she needed to win back some privileges so she could make a better plan.

Many weeks later found her in an all-stone, cold room, naked, in shackles, laying on the floor in a pool of her own blood. All possible plans were complete failures. She was broken in more ways than one.

He had repeatedly raped her, beat her, carved into her, and the last event, the most horrid, had him over top of her with something that caused so much pain she couldn't even comprehend. All she knew is she couldn't see out of one eye, nor open her mouth more than the size of a straw.

She also knew she had many broken bones, and her left cheekbone was certainly fractured, maybe even shattered. She didn't know how long it had been since that particularly awful experience, as consciousness was not a stable state, but the pain in her face was extreme. She couldn't even bring herself to think about what he had done, the moments of consciousness where she was aware of his actions so horrifying. Even starting to consider the memory had her eyes rolling into the back of her head, resulting in dry heaves or vomiting, depending on her diet for that day.

She only had one plan left. There was a small hope, but in truth the plan would probably kill her. Without any other alternatives she had no choice, and her body was telling her she was running out of time. She had resigned herself to understand his objective that if Richard couldn't have her, then no one would.

CHAPTER ELEVEN

Meanwhile in Memphis, Denny and Jessie were beside themselves. The police had arrived and they were trying to explain their concerns, provide pictures, possible contacts, and leads. It took quite a bit for the police to become concerned when the record label didn't seem to think anything was awry, stating that Raven liked to write songs in private and with the tour around the corner they expected to hear from her any day.

One man, Argus Sheffield, stated that he had just talked with Richard and they were on vacation at some private romantic location. Denny and Jessie exclaimed that there was no way this was possible. Raven would never do such a thing, especially not without telling them. After many demands, the police agreed to put a BOLO out for Richard and Raven, but Denny and Jessie weren't convinced they were putting a huge effort into that mission.

Many hours later, just as the sun was coming up, Jessie screamed, "I got it, I got it! Stupid, stupid Jessie! Why didn't I think of this before?"

She stood up from the table where they had been sitting and went running into another room. She returned moments later with a box clearly labeled HIGH SCHOOL and, while Denny had no clue where she was going with this, began to help her unpack the box.

"What are we looking for?" asked Denny. "I think the current photographs they have should work better than these, right?" holding up an assortment of snapshots from days gone by.

"No, no, not photos. The cigar box, there!" she exclaimed as she pulled the elongated wooden cigar box from the bottom of her school day treasure box. "Oh God, please let this work. Please," prayed Jessie as she dumped the cigar box contents onto the table and there it was . . . the heart locket. She had forgotten all about it, but now picked it up like a piece of precious gold.

"Science Fair, junior year, where's the disk. The disk? Where is it?!" Jessie demanded to the box as Denny flipped through photographs and letters.

"Like a CD disk?" asked Denny.

"God no, Denny. CD's weren't even invented yet . . . diskette. Here! Found it!" she exclaimed as she ran to her computer and popped it into the external USB drive she had been given by the hospital. This very moment being the only time she was happy about accepting the job of transferring old health data.

"Jessie, what are we doing?" demanded Denny, not wanting to waste any precious time. Three months. Where had his baby girl been for three months? How had he not realized he hadn't spoken with her? He was angry at himself. He knew the answer. He had been self-absorbed in his new life.

"What are we doing?!!" he demanded a second time.

"GPS. Remember? She made you one too so she would know where you were, but they confiscated it in your mail saying no soldier could wear an unsanctioned tracking device," she spouted as she clicked away at the keyboard, trying to remember how to initiate the program.

Denny vaguely remembered what Jessie was talking about, but more importantly was the burning question, "So she has a locket like this, and there is a GPS locater in it? How do you know she has it with her?"

"I don't, but she used to keep it in her makeup case. She said it was the one way she could carry home with her wherever she went. There! Look!" Jessie exclaimed as the software started to track the distance between lockets, finally drawing an arc line between their location and somewhere in Connecticut.

"Connecticut?" said Denny, having no recollection or clue about any person or place in that state. Still, it was the best lead they had. Denny picked up the phone to call the police again while Jessie booked them flights. There was a flight headed out in less than three hours. Come hell or high water, they would be on that plane.

After sharing the coordinates with the police who agreed to pass the information along the law enforcement highway, Denny and Jessie rushed to the airport. And, at that very moment, Raven was given the opportunity to put her last game play into action.

CHAPTER TWELVE

"Good morning, Sweetheart," said Richard as he kneeled to brush the hair out of her eyes, "Are you happy to see me?" When Raven nodded he asked, "So what do you want to do today?"

Mustering all her strength and ignoring the pain that came with talking, she pleaded silkily, "Sweetheart, I'm a little cold. Could you carry me up to the fire and lay on the rug with me? "

Beaming at the endearment and the idea, he jumped up like a little boy who just received a new bike, and did as she requested. As they proceeded into the cozy little room with the burgundy sofa and stone slab coffee table, she played out the scene she had rehearsed over and over in her head. After getting settled on the rug, and Raven getting as comfortable as she could possibly get, she began the plot.

"Do you remember that trip through Georgia where the bus broke down and the two of us walked all those miles to get to a phone? Was nice back then, kind of like now, with no one to bug us or interrupt our day, no cell phones. So peaceful. Just the two of us," Raven whispered, articulating as best she could, moving only her lips.

"Mmmmm, that was a good day," Richard whispered in her ear, leaving Raven with the most difficult task of not shuddering. "Do you remember what we did while we waited for the mechanic?"

"We played hangman, didn't we?" asked Raven softly.

"No, well we did. I was talking about how your feet hurt so bad from walking all that way in those ridiculous shoes," chuckled Richard, obviously enjoying the memory. "You said that was the best foot massage you had ever had."

"It was indeed. How I loved those stupid shoes," Raven agreed silkily. "And I don't know, I think I would need a repeat performance to confirm it was the *best* I have ever had. You've hired some pretty fine masseurs for us on the road," Raven whispered nonchalantly, slurring her words.

Unable to resist the challenge, Richard changed his position to instantly comply. He stretched her legs and as he touched the top of her right foot, she winced noticeably.

"I'm so sorry, Raven. I just love you so much. Look what you made me do; but, all of that is past us now, yes? You understand now, right? I did it for your own good, so you could see," Richard almost pleaded.

"It's okay, sweetheart, I know." As Raven winced again he asked if he was pressing too hard, a question that actually almost made Raven laugh, but she forced herself to stick to the script. Continuing, she whispered throatily, "No, your hands feel amazing. It's just the shackles. They're a little heavy." Raven laid back and closed her eyes, doing her best to look relaxed and forcing back the scream that wanted to say, *"Take the effin' things off of me!"*

Please God, please let him fall for his own manipulation tactics.

Richard rubbed her feet for a few moments more before she felt the first shackle slide off, and a few moments later the second. Resisting the urge to jump and run, Raven reminded herself there was nowhere to run to. Despite her four-week course in self-defense training, it had been proven time and time again that hand-to-hand combat would leave the win to Richard . . . and, at this moment, there wasn't much fight left in her. *Patience.*

The foot rub lasted about a half hour, Raven guessed. She was focusing on breathing in and out, nothing more, ignoring the pain, waiting for it to be over. Upon its conclusion, Richard returned to his spooning position on the rug, propped up on one elbow, the flames of the fire casting shadows on his face. *Patience, Raven.*

After about ten minutes of comfortable silence for Richard and a long-lasting tortuous silence for Raven . . . *breathe in and out, Raven* . . . she faked a slight cough, which was actually quite painful to do.

"Are you all right? Can I get you something?" Richard asked attentively, playing right into her plan.

"Could I have some water?"

As he left the room, Raven rolled and reached forward to turn the gas on the fireplace all the way up. She hoped the chimney hadn't been cleaned in as long as it looked. If the second part of the plan worked, the fireplace would be of little consequence, but just in case. Now for the hard part, she had to stand up and make it to the kitchen.

Holding onto the kitchen doorframe, and trying to hide that fact, Raven attempted a smile that only affected half of her face. "Wow, babe, you built an amazing fire. It's roaring," taking the plastic glass from his hands to drink thankfully.

"It's a gas fireplace, I just turned it on," chortled Richard.

"Really? I've never heard of that," said Raven, trying to smile again.

"Huh, I'm not surprised. You don't know how to boil an egg. That's one of the many, many reasons you need me," flirted Richard, moving closer, his eyes beginning to smolder.

Oh God. Running only on adrenaline she walked past him and said, "But I do know how to make coffee, and you love my coffee. Set me up and go put on something more comfortable. Those aren't lazy-day-laying-around-the-fire clothes. C'mon. Coffee, filters, scoop?"

By now Richard was looking at her curiously, but seemingly so overjoyed that his reprogramming efforts appeared to have finally succeeded, he complied without question. Even though Raven was watching surreptitiously, she failed to see where the key came from. Richard somehow had gotten a single key into his hand that unlocked the cabinet over the coffee maker where the necessary items were retrieved and placed on the counter, and cabinet relocked.

It was the first key she had seen. It was not on a ring as she had hoped. Feeling some dismay, she turned to prepare the coffee, shooing him out of the room. She prepared the filter and scooped in the coffee while listening to his footsteps move down the hallway. As soon as a door opened in the distance she hobbled to behind the stove, leaned on the tubing to the gas line until it detached, and turned the valve all the way up before finishing the coffee preparations. Turning on the electric pot, she limped back to the den as quickly as the pain allowed to initiate the next phase of the plan.

When Richard returned, she was over in the corner studying the music selections and an old worn-out turntable. The plan was a little fuzzy at the moment and her head was getting fuzzier right along with it. All she knew was that she needed to bide more time. Seeing a couple of albums that had memories attached, she called Richard over to share them and make a choice, the entire time making sure his back was to the fireplace where the flames had started to climb up inside and ignite the chimney dirt.

"I choose this, because I know it is your favorite," Richard claimed as he handed her an album of classical pieces, including the last selection, Pachelbel's *Canon in D.*

Perfect, thought Raven, seeing the first numbers on the music index. They would never make it to her favorite and apply the tarnish of the day's events to its memory imprint.

"Can you help me? I'm not sure how to do this anymore," Raven said as innocently and helplessly as she could, buying more time as he placed the album on the turntable and Tchaikovsky's 6th Symphony and probably his darkest, "Pathetique," spilled into the room. *How appropriate.*

"Thank you," said Raven, placing a hand on his arm and continued with, "Coffee is probably ready. I want to look through the rest of these really quick and see if I can find something a little more romantic for later."

"I'll get the coffee," Richard volunteered, kissing her naked shoulder.

"Oooooh, you know what else would be good? A cigarette, do you have any?" asked Raven, making her shudder look like excitement before changing her position to keep his back to the fireplace.

"Of course, I do. Coffee and a cigarette coming up," promised Richard as he strutted out of the room. Raven knew Richard would light it and take a hit or two. It was a control thing. He did it for her all the time and she hated it. Of course, today she hoped he wouldn't change his spots and assumed that he would want to keep her away from the locked-away lighter, and light it in there; but, how could she be sure?

In addition to that concern, she had no idea how long a time period was needed to make this work. Were we talking flint-like sparks or a Die Hard movie-type building explosion? It was not like she had ever rehearsed this. Did she need to extend the plan? Just about anything that would burn was bolted down, and books and album covers wouldn't do it. She could, however, yank the drapes, light an end on fire, and throw it on the books. It would be slower than her current plan, but it was a decent back-up compared to her recent failures.

Her answer came soon enough though, and although it wasn't enough to crumble the massive building, the explosion was powerful enough to knock her off her feet.

"Get up Raven," she screamed at herself. "Get up!" Half crawling, half walking, she pointed herself in the direction of the safest room in the house, Richard's favorite prison as of late. Focusing only on her pathway, she was caught off guard by Richard running into the room with flames shooting off his back and coming right for her.

"You Bitch!" he screamed at the top of his lungs as he swung her around by her hair.

This is it, Raven thought. Don't hold anything back, and she didn't. Her moves might not have made Jackie Chan proud, but her commitment to the fight would have. Finally, one lucky punch landed her fist with full force under his chin. That combined with the burning flesh on his body slowed him down and dropped him to his knees.

Raven used the lower height to her advantage, took a deep breath and exhaled slowly, ignoring the pain throughout her body. With great effort, she landed a hitch-kick squarely in the middle of his face. Blood splattered everywhere as he fell backwards against the stone slab coffee table, hitting the side of his head on the unrelenting decorative piece, before crumpling to the ground motionless. Raven, surprised she was even able to complete the move, also ended on the floor.

Crawling to his side, she was overwhelmed with despair when her clumsy search revealed no keys. The smoke in the house was unforgiving, just as unforgiving as the pain caused with each cough and gasp for air.

Unable to stand, Raven crawled to her planned retreat, fueled only by the desire to survive. A precarious slide down the stairs rolled her body into the all-too-familiar stone dungeon; and, with one final burst of energy, pushed the door closed using the weight of her entire body. She knew the stone room would either save her or smolder her, but one way or another this nightmare would end. Rolling away from the heat of the door, she lay in the center of the room and prayed for Heavenly intervention.

CHAPTER THIRTEEN

Denny and Jessie arrived in Connecticut about mid-morning and headed directly towards the coordinates. The kind stewardess had informed them that the State Police were waiting to escort them directly to the site, which both surprised and pleased Denny; although, of course, it worried him too. For a moment he feared the worst, but he couldn't let his mind go there. He chose to believe only that the GPS coordinates had inspired them to take the situation more seriously.

Arriving at the little twenty-four/seven diner that resembled a train car, additional State Police were already there questioning the young waitress sporting the locket around her neck. Jessie, seeing the locket, immediately ran up and yanked the precious jewelry off the girl's neck.

"Where did you get this? Raven would never give this away! What did you do to her?" shrieked Jessie, finally bursting into tears. A gentleman in uniform moved forward between the two ladies while Denny comforted her as best he could, looking white as a sheet himself.

The young girl, named Becky according to her uniform tag, looked to be in her early twenties and had tears in her eyes.

"It was a gift, I swear!" the girl defended herself. "Carl, the busboy, he gave it to me months ago. He's on his way here, I'm sure of it. His shift starts in fifteen minutes. I don't know where he got it, I swear! And this girl, these people, I've never seen them in here," she said, pushing the pictures back across the table top covered in graffiti.

Ten minutes later, Carl was being escorted into the diner from his car to the booth, where there were still more questions than answers.

"Hey, did you see the smoke? There's a fire somewhere," he told the men in uniform, still oblivious and seemingly uncaring as to why the young deputy was holding him by the forearm. But as he was shoved into the booth the young man expressed, "Hey, what's going on here?"

"The locket, Carl, where did you get the locket?" cried Becky before anyone else could make the official opening statement.

"What? I told you. I bought it on my trip," said Carl but his eyes were not as convincing as his words which had Denny jumping forward.

"Listen here, you little punk. You tell us where you got this right now or I will do everything in my power to put you behind bars and make your life miserable for the rest of your days," exclaimed Denny with unswerving eyes.

"Sir," the young police lieutenant who seemed to be in charge intervened, "please remain calm. Carl, the truth. Where did you get the locket? Answer me or I will arrest you for impeding a police investigation."

Looking at Becky with chagrin, shame floating in front of the puppy dog eyes he had for her, Carl exclaimed, "Okay, okay. I got it out of the dumpster around back. I was taking out the trash and there was a bunch of good stuff in there that someone had thrown out. The locket was in there too. I'm sorry, Becky. I just wanted to give you something special. I didn't want you to know I got it out of the garbage."

At that moment, another policeman ran into the room as sirens filled the air. "The boy was right. Fire up the hill. We gotta go."

The lieutenant turned to Denny and was about to push off the remainder of the meeting until after the untimely crisis; but, Denny didn't give him the chance.

"You get me up there right now. My Goddaughter is in that house, I just know it."

On the way up the mountain, Jessie and Denny's hands were clasped tight, praying for the best, leaning on each other. Jessie was seeing flashes of her dear friend, times they had spent throughout their life. The news of Raven's belongings being found in a dumpster, and her wondering if her friend had also been treated just as worthlessly, had zapped her of all strength.

Denny was also lost in a negative field of emotion. Trying to gaze through the smoke, anxious to get to their destination. He couldn't get the nightmares Raven had had as a child out of his mind. . . her waking up, covered in sweat and fear, screaming that she was on fire.

Shortly after, as Denny and Jessie moved closer, Raven thought she heard something different. Different was good. *Different is good.*

"Thank you, Lord," she whispered, as she passed out again, relaxing slightly for the first time in months, leaving her fate in His hands.

The next moment of consciousness contained an unfamiliar voice, "Miss? Raven? Oh my God, in here! We need a medic! Medic! Medic!!! You're safe now. You're safe now. You're safe now, breathe. Breathe! That's it, keep breathing. Stay with me. You're safe," and slowly, so slowly, she faded back into the darkness.

CHAPTER FOURTEEN

"Raaaven," whispered Fred in her ear, "you don't have to go home, but you can't stay heeeeeere."

"Well, that's not true," Wally interjected giggling, "She could if she wanted." Wally had been entertaining himself for the past half-hour while Raven slept with her head on the bar, drawing stick figures and doodle designs all over her hands and arms in different color markers. The most prominent message was *"We love you, Raven"* on the back of both of her hands.

Fred inspected Raven's arms musing, "You're quite good at that."

Wally was nodding and agreeing wholeheartedly, surveying his work with pride before picking up the sweater she had discarded from the floor at her feet.

They had already cleaned up for the most part, the last of the regulars had gone home. Michael, the only teenager allowed in after curfew, had captured one last video. It was of Wally the Artist, while Raven slept at the bar, looking like a curly-headed mop on top of her slender body. No one considered brushing the hair off her face, although Fred and Wally did discuss how difficult it must be to breathe under there.

"Good one, little man. Just don't stream that one, okay?" said Wally as the boy made for the exit grinning, heading for the car where his mother was waiting outside. His departure left the three of them alone, with Denny in his office finishing up.

Fred was wiping down the last of the bar and Wally was putting his markers away when, to their surprise, Raven jumped to her feet. Her stance said she was ready to attack. She was looking around like a wild animal running from danger. Her arms raised with strength and conviction, as if protecting herself from an unknown assailant.

"Whoa!" exclaimed a startled Wally, just as Denny shut his office door and walked into the front part of the bar. Denny had seen that look before, but not in a long time.

He quickly said, "Raven, wake up. You're safe, You're safe." Raven turned in the direction of the voice, still not seeing the room in front of her, and still resembling a wild animal in distress. "You're safe, Raven," repeated Denny over and over again in a low, calming voice.

And then, with the blink of her eyes, she woke. Seeing her arms, still held out in front of her, stopped her dead in her tracks.

"What the heck happened?" she asked laughing in astonishment at the artwork covering them. "Who did this?"

Surveying the room for the guilty party and catching Wally's eyes, she found her answer. Wally, of course, ducked agilely behind the bar. The dish towel thrown at his head not even coming close to hitting its mark.

"Hey, where did everybody go?" asked Raven, looking around, still a bit confused and unaware that she had been lost in her own world before finally falling asleep over two hours ago.

CHAPTER FIFTEEN

Thursday morning coffee at Bear Crossing Cabin no. 11 had become a regular weekly ritual, starting that first morning Raven had awakened in her newly remodeled home.

And, since Raven had started performing on Wednesday nights, she found herself exhausted enough to join a more normal sleeping pattern with the rest of the crew . . . at least on Wednesday nights. Despite the topic of conversation that ensued every Thursday morning, she loved waking to the smell of fresh coffee and at least two people in the kitchen.

Usually Fred and Wally were first. Fred would cook and Wally would read the paper, using the situation to practice his many dialects. Occasionally you would hear Fred call out a different dialect like some game show challenge. This morning Raven woke to Fred laughing at the previous scene and shouting "Jamaican," as Wally looked for the next interesting story to share as a Jamaican.

"Ya Mon, let's jeeest looka here, Mon. Goot to be a story worthy of eh gooood Jamaica!" A few paper-shuffling moments later, "Cho, Mon. Nuh ha nutten. Oooo, Cooh Deh! 'ere ee go, callaloo, Mon. Fawty cents ah pound, deh ah!" he said, finding a supermarket ad suiting his current purpose.

"Callaloo?" Raven mumbled as she walked into the room, bundled up in the afghan she had used to cover herself on the couch the night before. Like Open Jam Wednesdays and Coffee Talk Thursdays routine, Raven had grown accustomed to crashing on the couch in her clothes, like a temporary resting spot to just close her eyes before the gang arrived in the morning.

"Spinach," Fred explained without turning around, focusing on turning his pancakes with a fancy flip as she plopped down in her favorite chair, like the gravity of the room was just too strong for her. She was not yet awake enough to appreciate the graceful, athletic nature of Fred's cooking savvy.

"Coffee's hot," said Wally, as he pushed his half-empty coffee cup forward on the table. A not-so-subtle request for service.

Fred turned around to ask what kind of eggs each wanted as Raven reached for the presented coffee cup, allowing the afghan to drop behind her on the chair. As the three of them caught sight of her multi-colored arms, canvassed in Wally's artwork, there was a combustion of laughter that literally had Wally falling out of his chair and tears spilling out of the corners of his eyes. The sight of this, of course, made Fred and Raven laugh even harder.

The unstoppable laughter was interrupted as Denny and Marna swept into the room, hanging their coats on the handy hooks Denny had installed just inside the back door.

"What's the big joke?" smiled Denny, "You started the party without us?"

Raven had made her way to the coffee pot, still fighting the full-body laughter as the pair entered. Turning now to face them, no explanation was needed. Marna started giggling hysterically at the sight before her, while Denny shook his head, full of mirth.

Raven was still in her jeans from last night, in the tank top that was layered under her sweater, with wild hair sticking up in every direction. There was not a single inch of skin on her arms, not covered in multi-colored doodles.

"Hey, what can I say? Wally's here to entertain you at my expense!" Raven giggled, bowing to her beautiful bronzed friend as she served him his coffee. Returning immediately to the large pot and filling cups for the others, the only one left to arrive was Michael.

A lot had happened for Michael in the one month since the initial Jackson Hole video debut had been released. He was so excited when Raven suggested he continue his action lessons on Wednesday nights, along with some other assignments. The truth was going to come out; it always did. And Denny and Jessie were right. She did get a raw deal. Hiding from what she was born to do was no kind of solution for anyone, anywhere; and, not offering Michael this educational opportunity because of her baggage one hundred percent conflicted with her selfless nature. As it turns out, the suggestion changed Michael's life; and, as Raven would reflect later, changed her life too.

Michael, a senior in high school, had been struggling with boredom. With above-average intelligence for a young man his age, little studying was needed for his required courses. Having taken heavy class loads his first three years, Michael's senior year was filled with a lot of electives and study halls, along with the opportunity to join a vocational work release program. He had not done so at the beginning of the year, as most of the work release options were mechanical in nature, none of which appealed to this tech-savvy teenager.

It was actually Denny and Anna, Michael's mother, who came up with the idea. Anna was a single mother who worked many long hours. No one really knew what happened to Michael's father; and, respecting their privacy, no one asked. Anna and Michael had moved to the Jackson Hole area about the same time Denny had purchased the property, shortly before the time of Raven's hostage experience. It was Anna who came to Fred's aid on the many, many trips Denny had made to Memphis so many years ago.

When Denny hired Anna, he knew they were a good fit; and, unfortunately, also knew it was temporary. In one conversation with her, you could see that Anna was born to do greater things. "Not that there was anything wrong with being a waitress," she would have said in response to that statement.

Anna's generous spirit was no secret. She was known by everyone in town. Hard to not know Anna. She was now managing the Jackson Hole Daily, the newspaper the locals lived by. She had had many occasion to print stories that would have left negative imprints on people's lives, but those stories would not come from Anna's press. She had a way of presenting the facts, both positive and negative, without betraying the dignity of any one individual. She called it responsible journalism with a dash of kindness. These same skills were required by her reporters.

As an example, another paper might have taken advantage of the video footage in her son's hands. The *Jackson Hole Daily* could have run with a number of stories, sold many more papers and maybe even gotten national attention; but, the music headline did nothing of the sort. The Open Jam was reported as normal, although it did cover a very sincere welcoming to one of Jackson Hole's newest residents to their family stage.

Anna had an excellent skillset for detail and memorization. If she saw it once, she could remember it: faces, names, written facts, details. It didn't matter what it was, Anna could repeat it to you almost verbatim. Perhaps this skillset assisted her in raising a young teenage boy on her own, one that respected the truth and understood the definition of being honorable.

Because of Anna's reputation, along with Denny's eternal "Pops" personality, Michael had plenty of adult guidance, despite Anna's work commitments. The paper had even done a piece on how it *takes a community to raise good children*. Since that day, Michael kind of became the poster boy for community parenting, and he thoroughly enjoyed it.

From what Michael had shared, his early years had been secluded to contact with only his very intelligent mother. Perhaps that, and his own unusually high IQ, made him more comfortable around adults. And, not having a father, he reveled in every opportunity to help build a fence, put up a mailbox; and, every once in a while, you would find him over at the park throwing a baseball with Mario, who had no sons of his own.

It was also no surprise around the local community to walk in and see Michael behind a counter somewhere. When someone called in sick or extra assistance was needed, Michael would fill in willingly. Needless to say, Michael was a jack of all trades; but, in shooting the videos and working with Raven on the computer, he had found something he loved.

Anna was thrilled to meet Raven; and, although she remembered Raven was the reason Denny needed the many leaves of absence from Denny's Den, she had never mentioned it. Not even in the article that printed a week after her arrival, "Say Hello to Jackson Hole's Newest Resident," something she did for every newcomer, no matter how brief or extensive.

Some residents' interviews took up a whole page and some took up a single paragraph. Anna's sensitivity had proven to make everyone feel welcome, including Raven. Their interview had focused on how she liked Jackson Hole and working at Denny's Den. She also added information about Raven's computer skills, suggesting anyone needing help with a website, or other custom business solution, contact her immediately for quality work.

At the close of their interview, it was Anna who asked Raven for Michael's computer lessons. Recognizing her son's boredom in school, perhaps this would provide an outlet. Raven agreed, but would accept no compensation. The deal was that Michael would trade hour for hour. For every hour that he spent training with Raven, he would work for Denny. As Michael well knew, this could mean anything from sweeping floors at the bar, to fixing the plumbing in one of the cabins at Bear Crossing; and, he was thrilled.

Anna visited the bar for lunch often, Denny sitting down with her at least once a week to catch up with his good friend. The day after Michael's first streaming video release, Anna rearranged her schedule for one of those luncheons. Anna hadn't seen Michael since the morning coffee talk at Raven's, so she didn't realize that all was well. When Denny reassured Anna that everyone was fine, including Michael, relief washed over the kind woman's face.

"Oh, thank goodness. He has been so excited. He loves this so much that I hated to think he wouldn't continue," a concern pushed into her mind that morning as a distraught Michael left the house claiming he would never shoot another video again. It was a rare teenage moment for her son.

"Hi Anna!" said Raven, walking up with her lunch platter just in time to hear the last comment. "No! He can't give it up. He loves it and he is great at it! Sorry, waitress hazard, unintentional eavesdropping."

Anna laughed at the girl she found to be quizzically comical, assuming much of the comedy came from the need to avoid serious topics; or, perhaps an attempt to avoid all seriousness of life completely.

"I'm so glad you think so, Raven, and so sorry if anything Michael did upset you."

"Michael? Not at all, Anna. He is an amazing young man, and his motives are always sincere. That's what counts," stated Raven in a matter-of-fact tone. "You know, I've been thinking about him all day too. I think he is ready for an actual project of some kind, something solid that has a specific objective."

Denny chimed in, "What about the paper, Anna? Your online version could use an overhaul," he said, nodding at her with eyebrows raised.

Anna laughed, obviously reminded of days when the shoe had been on the other foot. She had helped Denny get his new business settled and organized with similar frankness.

"So true! It is a sad representation. You know, that is really the only complaint we receive? Honestly, I ignored it for a while because I like to hold the paper in my hand, but times have certainly changed. What do you think, Raven?"

"Well sure, that could work. We can revamp your navigation structure using something Michael designs, and both approve, of course. Maybe add a search function that actually works?" grinned Raven, relieved to see Anna smiling as she rolled her eyes, confirming her knowledge that in this area the paper had really been dropping the ball.

"We can install an interface for your staff to upload their articles and then maybe Michael can focus on bringing extra attention to the music section, especially since he has already entered the arena with a bang!" A suggestion that resulted in a table-wide chuckled agreement.

"So, like an internship for your paper with the two of you being his mentors? Anna helps him with direction of content, and Raven helps him adapt the content to the web," suggested Denny, spinning the plan to action.

"You know, if he started by focusing on the live entertainment here, which is the heart of the locals anyway, Denny and I could keep an eye on him. Make sure he gets home alright when you can't pick him up. Plus, we could also help him with suggestions as he does his work. And Denny, the live music page on your site, why don't we spice that up too?"

Anna was nodding and you could see her wheels turning. "You know what? I'm going to talk to the school. He turned down the opportunity for vocational training and work release because none of the topics suited him. I bet we can get the school to approve this as a work release program. Not only would he then get credit for the training and resulting work, he could also put that on his résumé.

"Not to mention, he would have more control over his school schedule. Poor Mario had to spend twenty minutes on the phone yesterday trying to get Michael released to work next door. Michael said he could hear Mario yelling in Italian over the phone from the corridor outside his study hall," laughed Anna as she shared the entertaining side note.

Mario was easily excited and, a long time ago, everyone learned that when Mario yelled, they should just take a breath and be entertained by the magic sound of his foreign rhetoric. He meant no harm. Because of this, when Michael reported to the office as requested, the old-timey telephone receiver was laying on the desk and Miss Shelly, the school secretary, was filing some papers giggling.

"He's really stressed out today, Michael! I already signed you out, but he wouldn't let me get a word in edgewise. So, he's all yours," she finished, nodding her head in the direction of the receiver bouncing slightly on the desk as Mario got louder.

"Apparently Michael didn't bother, he just asked Miss Shelly to hang up the receiver in ten minutes, giving him enough time to get over here!" concluded Anna shaking her head while Raven laughed at the idea of Mario still screaming into the phone when Michael tapped him on the shoulder.

After discussing a few more details about school policy and what needed to be done, Denny stood and prepared to get back to work.

"I think that is an excellent idea, ladies. Let me know if you need any help, Anna. We can draw up some sort of paperwork, if we need to, for the school or his work-release license, and also to be out after curfew on such a regular basis. I'll be happy to sign as his guardian here at nights and make sure he gets home at closing."

Placing a kiss on Anna's cheek, he returned to his office obviously happy about the chain of events.

"Anna, that's wonderful. I think Michael will be really excited. This interesting development with the first video could put him in front of some of the right people. If he wants to make a career out of it, you just never know what might happen," said Raven, looking around the bar to make sure no one was waiting on her. They weren't, but only because Wally was delivering food for her. He gave her the two-finger motion from eyes to eyes indicating he was watching her, and then of course shrugged her off that he had it covered. *Silly man.*

"Me too, Raven. Thank you so much. He has really changed since he started working with you. It has helped him get some direction. Seventeen can be such a scary age. I will let you tell him, because you can explain all *that stuff* much better than I can," admitted Anna.

"I know you need to get back to work, but Raven, between you and me, I remember all those years ago when Denny travelled to Memphis to stay with you. I realize what a sacrifice it might be to continue exposing yourself. Don't forget to do what's right for you too, hmmm? Now, enough of that," said Anna, patting her hand with two loving taps, knowing Raven well enough not to dwell on the last topic or expect a response. "I have to run. Great seeing you. I can't wait to hear what Michael says after you share the news!"

Michael had literally done a little jig when he heard the plan; and, he was still beaming that morning when he walked into Bear Crossing Cabin no. 11 with his laptop under his arm. The five people in the room couldn't be prouder of him. In the last four weeks, he had surprised them all with his fast work, logical ideas, and creative way of putting them into action.

He was making the transition from boy to man right in front of their eyes; and, for a first timer with regard to web and video work, his entertainment blog for the paper had a massive number of hits. It didn't hurt that Raven decided to continue performing on Wednesday nights. The conspiracy theorists were still comparing old notes, trying to get at the truth, all of them referring back to Michael's original posts.

So, Thursday mornings were now devoted to reviewing his work and enjoying the surrounding commentary. Raven didn't think his grin could get any bigger, but he managed it with one look in her doodled direction.

"If I knew you wouldn't kill me, a video of you right now would definitely go off the charts!" squeaked Michael, trying not to snort.

"Don't you dare!" laughed Raven, "I'd rather you Facebook what I had to eat today and you KNOW how I feel about that!"

Review of Michael's latest work received high marks from all. It was easy for everyone to see that he had the eye for video shots and the brain for video editing. He had gone from streaming live to putting together reels, all immediately upon returning home on Wednesday nights. Not only was he good, he was fast.

This development allowed him to separate the music of the evening into logical segments, providing both information about the musicians and commentary from the audience. Michael didn't really need the help, but the entire town wanted him to succeed. It appeared they were going the extra mile to make sure he had enough content for his online column.

Raven's section of Michael's blog was, of course, getting a bit more travel and talk time; but, Raven continued to honor her confidentiality agreement. Everyone in the room respected that decision. Michael, therefore, was treating Raven like any other artist at Open Jam, which Raven loved.

Anyone who knew Raven knew that it was about the music, and the music was enough. She enjoyed it even more when people shared it with her, but it was never about the notoriety. In all truth, the notoriety embarrassed her and the very reason her identity was originally hidden behind a costumed character.

Today the commentary review was more of the same old thing. Same questions, no answers. The only two differences Raven noted:

1) The question of the original Ravyn had now reached into the record label's social media accounts. Fans were demanding an answer; but, receiving no official response.

2) Musicmagic21, President of the *Kissed* Fan Club and the blogger that first made the connection, suggested that he might just have to make a trip to Jackson Hole to discover the truth himself.

Raven knew it was only a matter of time before *someone* visited her here in Jackson Hole with questions. Her location was no secret, especially since the *Jackson Hole Daily* had launched their new and informative website the week before. The address for Denny's Den was listed clear as day.

In truth, someone at the label or her former friends might have tried to contact her, but three days after the first video launched Raven stuck her old cell phone in a drawer and opened another phone account. The only people who got the new number were Jessie, Anna, and the five people currently occupying her kitchen. If anyone else wanted her attention, they would need to do it in person or in writing. Until then, she was protecting her solitude.

As Thursday morning breakfast and coffee talk had passed its climax and everyone had run out of jokes about the Ravyn conspiracy, the couple and non-couple said their congratulations to Michael; after which, they returned to their own cabins to prepare for work. Marna, of course, returned to her flower shop that had already been open for a couple of hours under the care of her trusty assistant, Cheryl.

Michael's new Thursday schedule meant he didn't have class until noon, working with Raven until 11:00. This morning Raven put him on the task of creating an image resizer for the paper staff console. Not understanding the idea of page load time, staff members were uploading full-size photographs, causing the pages to load very slowly. This new feature would help them upload their articles with the picture being optimized and resized appropriately in the process. Leaving him to it, Raven went to get dressed, needing a longer-than-normal hot shower to remove her excess doodle dirt.

CHAPTER SIXTEEN

Raven came running into *Denny's Den* at the very last minute like she had done since her very first day. With only a five-minute commute, she used every minute she could before beginning her shift. On Thursdays, that now meant coffee talk, working with Michael, and then a few precious minutes to play the piano, the latter being the one activity where she could really lose track of time.

Grabbing her apron from inside the stock room, she immediately began looking at the tables and the orders in progress. Making eye contact with Wally had them communicating in a sign language of their own design. Anyone watching would have wondered what the tall man was doing, but seconds later Raven was heading to Tables 3, 6, and 7 to take their orders. Also grabbing coffee on the way to refill Jacob's cup at Table 2, who, no surprise to Raven, was having the barbeque sandwich.

Raven's shift went as normal as could be until Denny finally came out of the office. By that time, food service was shutting down and cocktail hour was beginning. There was a normal lull around this time every day, 4:00 p.m., where only a few late diners might be finishing dessert, or a couple of locals were getting an early start on the evening shenanigans.

"Hey Denny! Where have you been hiding!" said Raven as she finished clean-up on Table 5 by pushing in the chairs.

"In my office," Denny smiled. "Don't need me out here with you and Wally in charge; and, Fred won't let anyone in his kitchen no matter how busy we get!"

"And truth be told," admitted Denny, "I was hiding from you," ending the statement by tapping a corner of the letter he was holding in the palm of his open hand. "I signed for this earlier. It's addressed to you."

Handing Raven the letter, he smiled and said, "When the paper site launched you said *ten days.* Not only do you have to deal with the letter, but you lost the bet. We all owe Marna a drink." Handing Raven the letter he motioned towards his office and said, "Take a few minutes. I'll cover for you out here."

Inside the comfort of Denny's office with the door shut, she sat in a brown tweed easy chair with her feet folded under her. The chair sported a fleece blanket on top, which added to the cozy feeling and offered warmth from the slight draft sneaking in the window. The office was just as comfortable as the rest of the place, and from her seat she could see the trees outside covered in snow, with the finest icicle gallery Raven ever witnessed.

Returning her gaze to the unopened letter, it was indeed from Diamond Back Records. Ripping open the seal and pulling out the monogrammed letterhead, she immediately looked at the signature. It was a name she didn't recognize. "Hmm," uttered Raven audibly as she began to read the content.

Dear Miss Reynolds,

It has been brought to my attention that you used to work with Diamond Back Records as the original "Ravyn" in our signed band, "Kissed." It was with utmost sadness that I read the confidential files relating to your employment with us; and, to say the least, Diamond Back did not treat you with the respect you deserved.

I am not aware of all the circumstances, but recognize you were physically unable to complete your signed tour through no fault of your own. I have also been privy to your private letters with the former CEO of Diamond Back, indicating your concern over your relationship with Richard, your former manager. As a female myself, I would have handled your concerns differently.

Since your time with our label, there has been a complete staff changeover. While we cannot repair the damage that has been done, we can perhaps offer a new direction. We would like to release you of your Confidentiality Agreement and stand with you as you tell your story.

I have had the privilege of seeing you perform on recent videos and can see what all the fuss is about, why your fans want to hear more. I would like to help you make that happen.

Looking forward to your response.

Kindest regards,

Angela Downey, CEO
Diamond Back Records

"Hmmm," said Raven again. The letter was not what she expected at all. Of course, she wasn't sure what to expect, but this letter never would have come from the male ego-oriented company that employed her so many years ago.

If this had been Raven's first rodeo, she would have been doing back flips, but it wasn't. Yes, this letter could be sincere, but at the same time it could have hidden motivation. If she did as Diamond Back requested, they would make a gold mine. Not only would it rekindle sales of the four albums released in her tenure, if she agreed to work with them, there would be new sales as well. And, with conspiracy surrounding the story, sales would be even higher. "Hmmm."

Unsure what to think, she slowly made her way back to the bar where she knew the three men would be waiting patiently for the latest news. Handing the letter to Denny with a shrug, Raven retreated to the waitress station to finish her prep for the following day.

As the letter made its rounds, they all had the same response as Raven, "Hmmm." Of course, Wally started with the blurt, "How did I not know your last name was Reynolds?" before adding his "Hmmm," to the collective thinking pot. Handing the letter back to Raven with the same shrug she had given to Denny, he broke into a huge grin and said, "You know what this means, right?"

At everyone's blank stare he announced excitedly, "Coffee Talk Friday!" After sharing a high-five with Fred, they disbanded from behind the bar and avoided the topic for the rest of the evening.

Coffee Talk Friday turned out to be not that eventful because Raven had already made up her mind. Today's gathering included just the four of them as the nature of conversation was a bit more personal, not to mention that Marna was running her own business and Michael was in school. As Fred set the fully loaded breakfast plates on the table and sat down to join them, they had all waited long enough.

"Well?" said the three of them almost at once.

"Well, I know what I'm going to do. Not all the details because I don't know what they will throw at me, but the gist. First, I want out of the Confidentiality Agreement, no strings. Second, *Jackson Hole Daily* gets the exclusive story and anyone else that is interested, including the label, must syndicate it from them. Third, if this Angela Downey wants a picture of us shaking hands, then she will have to come here. Fourth, there will be no cameras except Michael's. Fifth, I will not be returning to Diamond Back Records in any shape or form. And finally, no matter what happens, I will not be going on tour. If people want to see me, they will have to come to Denny's Den. Did I miss anything?"

"Sounds like a plan to me," said Fred, after thinking on it through a piece of bacon, the others also chiming in their agreement.

"Then it's settled. Denny, can you give me the name of your attorney?" When all three looked up from their plates with questioning eyes, Raven explained, "I'm going to want someone to look over these documents for me, to make sure it is a full release with no strings hidden in the language."

CHAPTER SEVENTEEN

Five days later found Raven, Denny, Michael, and Anna all sitting in an office waiting for Angela Downey, and Raven's new attorney, Dreyfus Miller, Esquire. It was still fifteen minutes before the scheduled meeting time. Raven was musing at the fact that the only one in the office that didn't seem to be nervous, was her. She had to admit, after speaking with Angela and Dreyfus on the telephone, they both sounded to be very nice people. She had higher hopes than the other three in the office, that this event would be drama free.

The room down the hall was prepared for the interview, with Raven and Anna having already agreed upon the questions that would be asked. Michael had set up multiple cameras, the official internship giving him access to better equipment. Denny was standing by to assist should he need help; and, of course, watch over his Goddaughter.

Dreyfus arrived first, knocking on the door. Upon being granted entry he looked around slightly frazzled, not sure he was in the right office. Placing his eyes on Denny, his complete expression and countenance changed. After exchanging a warm welcome with his former client, and now friend, Denny introduced Dreyfus around the room. Raven immediately stood to shake his hand and thank him for coming.

He smiled a terrific smile and said, "No problem, nice to finally meet you in person. After working with Denny as long as I did on your previous case, I kinda feel like we're old friends," he exclaimed, shaking her hand warmly.

Dreyfus was just getting settled into the chair next to Denny's, that also had easy access to a writing surface when another figure appeared in the open doorway.

"Raven?" the voice inquired as Raven stood up to greet her former record label's new CEO. Shaking her hand and offering formal greetings, the very short, stout woman said, "Call me Angela. The only Mrs. Downey I know is my mother."

Once again, introductions went around the room. After shaking Dreyfus's hand, Angela got right down to business.

"You will want to review these," the woman said with complete command as she took a stack of papers out of her briefcase. "I hope you don't mind. I've taken the liberty of putting an asterisk next to the clauses I think you should object to. Lawyers, they insist on these things," she explained to the room.

"Feel free to make your own decisions, of course. Those are just my suggestions," she grinned, handing him a bright pink pen before he could reach for his own. "You walk off with that baby and you will remember where you got it!" she jested.

"So, Raven, is everything in place? Happy so far?" asked Angela, who pretty much had given Raven control of all the proceeding details. Raven was distracted by Dreyfus crossing out clauses and Angela smirking as she caught him following her asterisk plan.

"Why are you doing this?" Raven asked bluntly.

Angela cocked her head to the side for a minute as she surveyed Raven thoughtfully. With a straight face and very formal manner, she finally broke the silence.

"Officially, as CEO, it is my duty to protect the company's bottom line. You know very well that's what I am doing, because you are a smart girl. This story, no matter where it is published, or what you decide to do next, will skyrocket sales of the four original *Kissed* albums. Off the record . . ." she hesitated, looking around the room for confirmation. After receipt of same, continued with a much softer tone.

"I may be the major stock holder of this company, yes, that would be me; but, I am also a compassionate human being. What happened to you, very simply, wasn't right. Sadly, I can't say yours is the only confidential file I have reviewed, but I can say yours was the most disturbing. Your concept, your work. You signed the original contract at nineteen, correct? Frankly, the devious, yes, I said *devious*, previous management took advantage of your naivety.

"Now, your Godfather and Mr. Miller here, they fought and won you back the rights from your original contract, which until that battle was dependent on you actually being on stage. Good job, Gentlemen. But, as Mr. Dreyfus is about to find out as he turns the page, there is a new sheriff in town. Now again, I can't fix the damage of the past, but I can make it right in the present. From this date forward, you will receive the proceeds you should have been provided at nineteen. So, in honor of signing this Agreement, I am also here to provide you with some of your back earnings, what I could adjust legally, along with a little extra as a small token of our apology. And of course, every quarter you will get a payout. I think you will be pleasantly surprised," she said as she reached into her briefcase and handed Raven a check for $300,000.

Gasps could be heard around the room. That was significantly more than the amounts received over the last nine years, as Raven had only recently discovered.

"Not nearly as successful as when you were in the band; but merchandising, downloads, ticket sales, all of it has a piece with your name on it. Again, your concept. Now, as I mentioned on the phone, we don't release our artist earnings so that part, and only that part, shouldn't leave this room. Agreed?" she asked again looking for confirmation.

"So, beyond that detail, there is no hitch?" asked Raven again.

Angela laughed in the most ladylike manner, a laugh that didn't seem to fit her body, but completely matched her friendly smile.

"No, my dear. No hitch. Of course, on a personal note. If you ever decide to work with a record label again, I hope you will think of me. In your shoes, however, I imagine a lot of trust will have to be earned before you cross that bridge. So, let's just agree to be friends and take it from there, shall we?"

Meeting Raven's gaze completely and unflinching, Raven finally relaxed and began to nod her head stammering, "Thank you. Really, thank you."

"My dear, I don't know what happened to you and it is none of my business, but you get back out there and do what you were born to do. Don't let anyone stop you or even give you directions. You'll find your way. Are you a Christian woman, Raven?"

A little overwhelmed by the events, along with the vivacious energy of the woman before her, she responded with a simple nod.

Angela mused for a moment that the girl in front of her looked like a wide-eyed, innocent teenager. How had she maintained that innocence after what she experienced? Yes, Angela actually did know what happened to Raven. There had even been photos and a police report in the file. While she was certain she didn't know the complete horror of it, what she had seen had been enough. However, she didn't feel it was her place to recognize that knowledge. If Raven ever wanted to discuss it, she would have to initiate the conversation.

"Then you really know what it means when I say I have faith," Angela said more as a statement than a question, causing a wide-eyed Raven to nod again.

"Your file came across my desk for a reason. It burned a hole there, beckoning me to take affirmative action. Imagine my surprise when I did some digging, trying to find you, and found young Michael's video. It was your first one, I think. The surprise exposé? I had already been working on your case for two weeks when that showed up, legalities and all. Had to cross my T's and dot my I's, you know. After that, it was just a waiting game. It took some time for me to work out all the pieces, and here we are. So, no matter what you decide to do, I have faith that it will all work out in the end."

At that moment, Dreyfus closed the stack of papers back to the beginning and said, "We're good. Let's get some signatures and we can move on down the road."

Over the next fifteen minutes Dreyfus reviewed everything with Raven, explaining why he crossed out the clauses as suggested by Angela. Once the changes were initialed and the signatures in place, they all relocated to the little studio Michael had set up down the hall.

"Might I offer a suggestion?" asked Angela, noticing that Anna looked more than a little nervous. When the question was answered by a chorus of agreement, she continued.

"Am I to understand that you two have prepared questions and answers; and, that you normally work with print, Anna, not video?"

"Yes," confirmed Anna, whose nervousness was apparent even in the simple, one syllable answer.

"And Raven, I'm guessing that while you are willing, and maybe even getting to the stage of *wanting* to reveal your past association, you are not too keen on an extended interview. Correct?"

Raven agreed, a bit in awe. Angela commanded the room with such ease, to no one's concern. She was considerate and kind; but, moving things right along. Her words and actions making sure all objectives were met and all parties agreeable. It was not hard to see how this woman could turn a company around. Denny was actually watching this woman thinking she would have made a great marine.

"May I read your script, please?"

After pausing for a cursory review, she continued.

"My suggestion would be to print your story. Provide the details in the manner you are most comfortable; and, allow me to get up there on video with Raven to make a formal apology from Diamond Back Records. It's not live, right? So, if you don't like it, or we need to tweak it to make it just right, we can do that? Just a suggestion of course. Neither of you look too excited at the moment, and I might be able to make this short and sweet. Shall we try?"

"Yes!" said both Raven and Anna simultaneously.

"I had an inkling," Angela smiled to Anna. "Okay, Raven. Over there. You want to be to my right, correct? Okay, and me over here. Michael, dear, do you need anything from us to get rolling? Maybe do a first take as a test of your vision, dear?"

"Yes Ma'am. Raven Reconnect Interview, Take One, Rooooolling," said Michael like a pro.

"Hello, ladies and gentleman. I am Angela Downey, CEO of Diamond Back Records, and I am here today with a very beautiful guest, Miss Raven Reynolds. You all might remember her as the original Ravyn from the band, *Kissed*. Raven toured with the band worldwide for six years, promoting the first four albums. Her last tour ended about nine years ago. Hi Raven, thank you for agreeing to meet with me."

"My pleasure, thank you for inviting me," smiled Raven, with her professional performance mask in place.

"I am here today to say that fans around the world, me included, are thrilled to find you on stage again. We do hope you will continue," she paused with a sincere look to Raven. "I am also here today to issue a formal apology to both Raven, and the fans of

Kissed. Previous management made decisions that are not agreeable to our current platform and we are doing our best to make it right.

"With that being said, Raven was involved in an incident that left her physically incapacitated. Instead of allowing Raven to recover and continue her work, the company secretly replaced the Ravyn character with the very capable, Elizabeth Tonkem. For nine years, Diamond Back has been maintaining that charade. It stops today.

"Now, for you *Kissed* fans out there, no need to worry. *Kissed* will be maintaining their regularly scheduled tour and Elizabeth Tonkem will maintain her position as *Ravyn*.

"For the burning question *here*, the future of our lovely Raven, that is for her to decide. I formally announce that she is welcome at Diamond Back Records, should she decide that is her wish; but, for now, we have agreed to just be friends. So, welcome back Raven!"

"Thank you, Angela, happy to be back."

"Now, if you would like to see Raven perform live, you have to come to Jackson Hole. A lovely little spot called Denny's Den. If you have been watching the up-and-coming director's blog, that would be young Michael Turnbilt, you know that Raven has been performing on Wednesday nights. As of today, I understand that has changed. Wednesday nights is now a closed evening event for the locals that live in Jackson Hole, you lucky folks. The rest of us will have to watch the video feeds on that night; however, Raven has agreed to perform for a few hours every Friday night, as well as a Gospel Brunch every other Sunday, correct?" asked Angela, looking to Raven for confirmation.

"That is correct, Angela. Hope to see you there," said Raven smoothly, as she had done in so many other interviews years before.

"Oh, trust me, I will be there this Friday. I expect it will be standing room only. So, if you want to join the fun, you might want to make a reservation. This can be done directly on the venue website or the *Jackson Hole Daily* website. Those addresses are now flashing across the screen. Once again, welcome back Raven. We wish you much success."

After a professional goodnight from the pair, they paused, smiling into the camera indicating the interview was over.

"Cut. That's a wrap!" This official statement from the young man made the entire room laugh, leaving Michael to say sheepishly,

"I mean, if you are happy with the content," as Denny proudly patted him on the back.

"Angela, how did you know about the new schedule? It's not even on the website yet?" asked Raven a little stunned.

"It was in the script, my dear," responded Angela nonchalantly, wowing Raven once again. She had glanced at it for like what, thirty seconds?

"Here comes the playback," said Michael, after punching a few buttons.

"That is marvelous, Michael! I think you are right. If Raven is happy with the message, that is a wrap. I would never have guessed you to pull that off on the first take. Brilliant," said Angela. "Everyone happy? Yes? Okay, good. How much time to choose the camera angles, fill in the green screen, and add the web addresses?" she asked, redirecting her attention to Michael.

Michael looked at Raven and grinned, prompting her to respond with, "Let's all go get some coffee."

Raven ushered them all out of the room, pointing to her cell phone. Michael would text her when he had a product to share. As they walked down the hallway towards the cafeteria, Angela wore an expression of confusion for the first time that day.

Denny looked at her smiling, beating Raven to the punch by responding, "The kid works fast."

"Oh!" exclaimed Angela, now understanding, "Nice. So, this could go live today? That kid's got a future for sure."

CHAPTER EIGHTEEN

Just under three hours later, Angela and Raven were following Denny and Dreyfus out of town and down the little road that led to Denny's Den. Angela, had a rental car and was staying at the closest hotel until Saturday. They both had accepted their invitation for a meal at the bar; and, as their personal guests at the local jam night.

The new "locals only" rule had been put in place at the request of Raven. She didn't want any of the press, curious tourists, or uninvited guests, disturbing the historic ritual. Maybe it was going overboard, overthinking, but then again . . . if no outsiders showed up in town, then the rule didn't really mean anything except to let the locals know that Denny's cared. Denny had considered the idea a simple win-win.

Michael and Anna both remained at the newspaper. Michael was finishing up his work on the video upload and press release while Anna returned to her daily duties, but both promised to see them all later that night.

During the drive back, Angela seemed to be bothered. "Is everything alright, Angela?" asked Raven, sensing her unease.

"There is something bothering me, Raven; but, I think we understand each other so I'm just going to be blunt. I made a promise to a few others before coming here today. I considered breaking that promise, because if I were in your shoes, I would want to leave it all behind me. But, a promise is a promise.

"First, the very persistent *Kissed* Fan Club would like to honor you by throwing a party. I've never met the President, but he has been around for a very long time and apparently has connections. He found out about our scheduled meeting here somehow and no doubt, the *Kissed* fans will join in that demand.

"Second, the ladies have also requested a meeting, well Jasmine, in particular, really wants to reconnect with you. My experience with Jasmine says she probably didn't have too much say in what went on all those years ago; but, I imagine, even knowing that may not change your feelings. It is your choice of course. Consider me as only the messenger."

"I will think about it," agreed Raven, who was lost in her own thoughts the rest of the short trip.

Jasmine had been the first friend she made at college. Her lack of self-confidence had been evident the very day they met. In fact, their meeting was a result of Raven, a bystander, instinctively swooping in to help the girl out of a rather intense conversation about her test scores setting the bell-curve for the class. She was a kind-hearted soul and wore that characteristic on her sleeve. So kind, in fact, she would rather take the verbal beating instead of pointing out the bully's own inadequacies.

It used to irritate Raven to no end that she let everyone walk all over her. For someone so powerful and commanding when playing the drums, her character, aptly named "Jasmania", and dressed as a Tasmanian devil, she was an absolute wimp when it came to handling everyday life. Her kindness was both her greatest strength and her greatest weakness.

Katrina, on the other hand, was as easy going as they came. She didn't let people push her around at all, but Katrina was a lover, not a fighter. She would find the easiest solution to stop any conflict and put it into action, albeit not always the *best* solution. However, her laid-back vibe transferred into her bass playing, which helped create the unique *Kissed* sound and feel, entertaining the audience as a hippie-vamped costumed character named *Kittee*.

And finally, Patti, the only one that insisted on picking her own name although her choice did unfortunately fit her personality: Python, on guitar and now lead vocals.

Python had always been a challenge for Raven, even in the early days. No one really knew her that well. When she was selected, it wasn't a long-term commitment. When the class project turned into something far greater, and so fast, Python's true nature wasn't revealed until it was too late, too complicated to make a switch. They weren't all bad times, but one fact was absolutely true. If there was drama happening within the confines of the *Kissed* tour, Python would somehow be at the center of it.

And another truth was that if Python had any chance to outdo Raven in anything, a big deal would be made of it. Python didn't like not being the first priority or the fact that Raven had more control than she did over show decisions. Raven had quickly given up the idea of changing the dynamic. The fact that Python needed the notoriety more than she needed the music would never change.

Relieved to be at their destination and focus her thoughts elsewhere, Raven hopped out of the car and led Angela into the warm, comfortable room that currently smelled like apple pie.

Once inside, Denny waved them over to a table and invited Angela to get situated, with Dreyfus facing the fireplace already looking at the menu. Raven, meanwhile, went to check on Wally and Fred, knowing full well they could handle things without her.

Wally, knowing that Raven didn't like to sit down on her shift, told her to take the orders from the outstanding tables, including her own, and then to sit down and enjoy her meal. Grateful to have an easy purpose for a few minutes, she complied before returning to the conversation already engaged at Table no. 8, Denny's favorite table for no solid reason he could give.

Approaching the table, she heard Dreyfus ask, "So what happened to Rusty?"

"He is now happily living in Cabin no. 3, the only one we now refer to as *Hunter's Cabin*," answered Denny.

"I don't understand," said Dreyfus, dipping his French fries in homemade fry sauce. "I offered you a couple hundred dollars to remove that poor animal from this bar last time I was here, what happened?"

"Right on cue, Raven," said Denny as she sat down. "Raven happened."

Laughing at Denny's face, Dreyfus exclaimed, "Way to go Raven! I can see who has the pull in this place."

The conversation that followed was friendly. Dreyfus shared information about his practice in Salt Lake and how he had moved out here just after college after living all his life on the east coast. But mostly he talked about how he spent his free time hiking and enjoying all that Utah had to offer.

Angela shared how she had always loved music and started on the road, some details about her life in New York, and how she had never expected to be where she was today. One day she just decided that if she wanted a label to do the right thing, she had to run it herself.

Both of their stories were captivating and Raven found she truly enjoyed these new friends; they were very interesting people. And even more importantly, she appreciated that throughout the entire conversation, not one mention was made about the true reason they were both here in Jackson Hole, at least not until Michael burst through the door with his laptop and a big grin on his face.

"It's done," said Michael, obviously excited that he had been able to meet the challenge. "And, in only one hour, it has received approximately 4000 hits!"

"Well done, Michael, well done!" applauded Angela, immediately pulling out her smart device and sharing it to the Diamond Back social media stream.

And with that news, Denny looked at Raven and reminded her, "What was that you said? Let the games begin?"

CHAPTER NINETEEN

In the weeks that followed, there were indeed many changes that occurred at Denny's Den; and, frankly, no one was sure how they felt about it. First and foremost, they needed help. Despite the way Denny's was designed for easy workflow with only a few staff members, they had to adjust.

Wally insisted that the cooler honor system would no longer work. He said, "If I don't know them, they can't be trusted."

You see, Denny had always had this dream of a local bar where everyone could come and feel safe; a home away from home. This was evident in how the bar was arranged. The largest oddity being the honor cooler. Basically, that meant if you wanted to drink something out of a bottle or can, you could get it yourself out of the cooler; and, of course put your money in the collection box: $1 for cooler one, $2 for cooler two, and $3 for cooler three.

Denny had bragged to Raven on her first day, "To date, we have only had six beers stolen. Not bad for ten years, eh?" There were cameras above the area as a precaution, but Raven wasn't convinced Denny even had them connected.

She didn't believe it at first, but now she had seen it with her own eyes. She had even seen one inebriated fellow start to walk away, simply forgetting in his over-relaxed state, and his buddy in about the same condition nudge him and point to the box. Jacob had come in more times than Raven could count asking the same question.

"Were you missing any beer payments last night?"

When Wally said that they were good, Jacob would stuff a $20 bill in the jar just in case. He recollected drinking the beer and was feeling the results of it the following morning, but just couldn't remember putting his payment in the box.

Truth be told, Jacob did forget often; but, every time he came in and put $20 in the jar, Wally would pull it out and put it on his tab. Jacob was up about $40, so he could forget a few more nights. It had even become one of the games before things got so hectic, each placing a bet on how many Jacob would forget that evening.

But things were different now, and it wasn't just due to Raven. Although there had been a significant number of new people showing up in old fan t-shirts from concerts past. Michael's blog had also gotten some attention for the other local musicians — Kevin, Randy, Seth, and the young alternative band. Raven could never remember their name, which means they needed a new one she thought every time that memory issue occurred. Even Bernie, now the infamous "Jugman," had developed a fanbase. So, Raven had invited them to share the stage with her on Friday. Raven played the first set with Randy, Seth, and Bernie, the same musicians that had shared the stage with her that first night. It was a jazz and blues cocktail hour, a theme requested by Denny.

The second set opened the stage to the young alternative group Raven had resigned to calling *Mashed,* because of the way they intertwined styles so eloquently with every song, both originals and covers. So, from 10:00 to 11:00 on Friday nights the bar filled with their young adult friends.

Previous open jams had required the youngsters be accompanied by an adult, preferably their parents, but this change required them to hire a doorman. The first couple of Fridays that it became an apparent need, Fred pulled out the stamp he had secretly used to make the Raven tattoos and took it to the door where Mario and Jacob had jumped up to assist. No stamp, no alcohol.

And the last set was an out and out party with all of the senior musicians on stage, Kevin and Raven exchanging leads and adding harmony where it felt right. Raven had been relieved that Kevin now seemed to have less bravado and had adapted into quite the team player.

This particular Saturday had the Bear Crossing crew looking less than fresh, frazzled by the frenzy of the days that had passed. Thanksgiving came and went almost without notice, with the little family saying their thanks over one of Mario's pies, too tired to even cook for a personal gathering. In fact, it had been so busy since the formal announcement, they hadn't even had time to really follow the commentary. Of course, with the secret out, and Raven being free of all her past concerns, there was no need to read it.

Michael, who was taking on more and more responsibility, however, was beginning to hound her about doing her own website and social media presence. He was right, but Raven had seen what turning music into a business could do. Was it possible to treat music as a business and it not lose any of its magic? Was it possible to be part of the fans' lives without losing her own sense of self?

Raven didn't have the answers to those questions, and frankly, had been distracting herself with other ideas. She was finally ready to share what she had been up to, so that Saturday at closing time Raven exited saying, "Breakfast on me tomorrow, Cabin no. 11. Don't be late unless you want to miss your surprise!"

An announcement that had Fred cocking his head at her quizzically while Wally jumped up and down, clapping, his eyes open wide in excitement, "I love surprises!"

CHAPTER TWENTY

The next morning was not a genuine impromptu gathering, her shout upon exit was just a reminder. Raven had already set up another basket delivery with Marna, which she insisted on paying full price for and Marna insisted on delivering for free. Giggling together they agreed. This arrangement had been made about a week before. Raven wanted this meeting on Sunday because everyone could be there and not worry about rushing off.

The Gospel brunches had been quite successful and very satisfying to Raven, who filled the hour mostly with gospel and Christian pop original tunes, and a few requests for some standards. Every once in a while, someone would chime in and lead some scripture or the thought for the day. Raven didn't talk much, except when the conversation really got interesting. Otherwise, she would turn to the piano sharing the sentiment, "I speak best through music."

But this Sunday was the off-day. Marna usually closed her shops on Sunday and another big snow drop had most thinking about skiing more than gift baskets or flowers. Raven's order had, in fact, been the largest of the week.

Anna had gotten her Sunday edition launched many hours before and had her Monday edition all prepped . . . barring any breaking news stories that required the standard shuffle. She had been thrilled to be invited to one of the infamous meetings at Bear Crossing Cabin that Michael loved so much, so she made sure all her ducks were in a row. Most teenagers would have rolled their eyes at their mom intruding on their gatherings, but not Michael. First and foremost, his mom was his best friend.

So, there they all sat in the kitchen with Raven in her chosen favorite chair, with her back to the counter and even though this place was her sanctuary, a clear view of all exits. Marna was to her right, sitting relaxed with her legs crossed. Her eyes were twinkling as they always did when Denny was near, and she had on the prettiest looped scarf that brought out the blue in them. Denny, in his customary red flannel, had his hands on the two spindles of Marna's chair and was leaning against the counter.

What would it take for them to see the light? Raven thought to herself as she had a million times before.

Across the table was Wally, beaming. A much shorter Fred was sitting comfortably and easily over one of Wally's legs.

"What?" said Fred at Raven's PDA surprise, something they didn't normally do. "You're cutting into our alone time and gave my man the morning off with your muffins!" he exclaimed, causing resounding laughter to which these kitchen walls were no stranger.

To Raven's left were Michael and Anna. Michael had pulled one of the chairs from the right of the entry way, just past the coat hooks. The sixth chair remained in place, ignored by Fred, obviously.

"We are just waiting for one more person," smiled Raven. "No Jessie couldn't come," said Raven at Denny's excited guess. Of course, the thought that Jessie had been invited increased their curiosity as to why Raven had called this meeting. The level of curiosity rose even more when a knock on the door drew their attention to a bundled-up Dreyfus, waving from outside the six-paneled window door.

"Come on in!" invited Raven as Denny waved to his old friend, greeting him cheerfully across the slightly crowded room. Michael jumped up to retrieve the final chair to provide Dreyfus a seat at the table.

"Ready?" Dreyfus asked as he smiled and winked at Raven.

"Ready!" Raven giggled in response.

Dreyfus had turned out to be an easy-going, caring person, unusual compared to the lawyers Raven had met in the past. They had conversed several times over the last several weeks to discuss the funds received. He had been the one to help Denny set up that funnel in the first place, so it was only natural that he would continue to help her. Raven was comfortable with that; plus, Denny trusted him. And as Raven knew, with the exception of the piano mistake that had actually turned out to be an incredible blessing, Denny's gut was never wrong.

"So," said Raven, so excited she could hardly contain herself as she watched a grinning Dreyfus pull their presentation items from his briefcase.

"First, Denny, we paid off your mortgage. Bear Crossing is now free and clear. We also put in a trust to handle the land taxes. It might have to be adjusted, but Dreyfus has agreed to keep an eye on that."

"Exhibit One!" exclaimed Dreyfus, putting the related legal documents in front of Marna and Denny on the table. Denny's mouth opened in surprise, but no words escaped his lips before she continued.

"Second, thanks to Anna knowing all the right people, we were able to purchase all the land in between the main road. So, when you turn off to go to Denny's Den, you are on your land. You can even put up a sign if you like. Dreyfus sketched up an idea he thought you might like and it is totally awesome."

"Exhibits Two, Three, and Four!" Dreyfus said as he laid them on the table for all to see. The first was a sketch of the exact turn-off revealing a clever set of Bear sculptures, one of them pointing with a sign dangling beneath that read "This way to Bear Crossing," The second showed an archway that would be a little further down the road. Across the top was written *Welcome to Bear Crossing.* All carved from wood, it was very fitting in the natural setting. And the third was a directional sign with a bunch of pointed arrows.

One sign said Denny's Den, one sign said Mario's Pizza Pies, one sign said Cabins, and the rest were blank.

"Coo dat!" said an ecstatic Wally, "but what are the blanks for?" His thought process making him falter out of accent.

"Well, Wally, I'm glad you asked that. In order for this deal to go solid at 5:00 p.m. tomorrow, we had to make some promises. First, we have to pave and maintain the road."

This bit of news brought cheers from both Marna and Anna, who both drove small cars like Raven's. The men, who all drove work trucks, grunted in jest and bravado at the ladies' cheers.

"Also, I told them we would work to become an entertainment and educational center that would make Jackson Hole proud. So, with that being said, we contacted an architect and he provided us with a few options."

She paused, grinning at Dreyfus, who promptly unrolled a blueprint of the entire land ownings of Bear Crossing, five square miles, including half the lake. He quickly and purposefully placed papers over certain areas of the map as he and Raven had discussed. Raven then began drawing their attention to the turn-off into Bear Crossing.

"Okay, all this can be moved around. We just did the best we could in the short amount of time we had to make the city board presentation last week," explained Raven.

"So that's where you were off to!" laughed Fred, shaking his finger at her. He knew she hadn't taken off work to go get a pedicure.

"This first building here is a gift and flower shop, Marna, with a sewing studio attached. You always said that your favorite love was to design clothes. Now you will have the tools to put that dream to the test. Plus, our new theater will need costumes made," she said as Dreyfus dramatically whipped up one of the pieces of paper to uncover the little building marked theater.

Before Marna's gasp could even leave her lips, Wally squealed.

"Oh no you di'n't!" He was so excited that he jumped up out of his chair, spilling an unexpecting Fred onto the floor. "Oh my goodness, a theater and what, will there be a theater troupe? What??! Oh, my goodness!" he exclaimed again, still doing a little dance.

"Slow down there Shakespeare," laughed Raven. "Before I answer that, do all members before me accept their position as a board member of Bear Crossing LLC? If so, say aye."

"Aye!"

"Those opposed say nay?" Silence followed this query of Raven's. "All board members who nominate Wally the head of all the Theater . . . er . . . *stuff*, raise their hands." All hands flew up without hesitation while Fred replaced himself in the chair. It was obvious Wally was not going to return to his seat, due to his excitement and continuing happy dance.

"I guess that will be up to you, Wally," Raven smiled.

Dreyfus, following Raven's finger, removed another piece of paper curtain. "A little further down the road we have a video and recording studio. Michael, I understand from your mother that even prior to us bringing all of this chaos into your life, you were planning to attend an online college and have already registered for next year, correct?" As Michael nodded, there was both fear and excitement in his eyes.

"All those who nominate Michael to manage the video department of Bear Crossing, under the guidance of all other Board Members until he graduates, at which time said vote will be placed for direct management, please raise your hand." All members raised their hands instantly and with mirth.

"And Fred, of course you get that kitchen upgrade you have always wanted," said Raven, causing Fred to jump up and join Wally, reinitiating the happy dance yet again. Denny was beaming, speechless with pride at what his Goddaughter was doing for them.

"And finally, over here, there is an area that we could get into additional rental cabins, but the only one that has to be built immediately is this one," Raven explained, pointing to a cabin a bit of distance away from the possible new cluster. "And the terms are that Denny, you help build it with your hands because you are the best," stated Raven, looking expectantly at Denny.

"What? Who would say that?" laughed Denny.

"C'mon Pops," defended Fred, "you know you are the best!"

"I would say that!" admitted Dreyfus.

Raven shrugged, "We need an attorney on staff. He can't be here full time, but with an adequate office space, it will make it easier for the rest of this to happen. So THAT actually is our first build." And with that, Raven sat back and looked at the crowd. "Too much? Everyone happy?"

The room filled with excited answers at once. Everyone was talking over each other, quite animated.

"Ladies and gentlemen, you have now been *Kissed*!" giggled Raven. "Merry Christmas!"

With Christmas still two weeks away, Wally stopped dead and looked at Fred, "We are going to have to seriously reconsider her Christmas gift," a statement of course designed for comedic effect that succeeded.

But the comment brought a puzzled look to Michael's face, which finally led him to say, "But Miss Raven, what do you get?"

"Isn't that obvious, Michael? I get all of you!" Raven said, hugging him with pure happiness.

Before they adjourned, they got down to the more immediate business of deciding how many people to hire at the bar. Two waitresses, a bar back, and Fred reluctantly agreed to let Denny help him cook, but only when absolutely necessary. The topics included handling the new additional traffic and other "boring stuff" as Wally called it. He was doing his best to concentrate, but all he could think about was which play would be first in his brand new, shiny theater.

CHAPTER TWENTY-ONE

Christmas time for Raven had never been so magical. The environment in Jackson Hole was the perfect winter wonderland, and the people that surrounded her all seemed to have laughter built in their DNA, like Santa Claus. That little Sunday afternoon meeting had kicked off the seasonal spirit for Raven and, from that moment on, she had Christmas carols blaring through the house.

Christmas Eve fell on a Friday with the bar closed on Saturday and Sunday. Raven was excited for the event; guessing the crowd would be small that night, as most people would be spending the holiday with their families. She hoped this was the case so she could focus more of her attention on the people closest to her.

But today was Tuesday and Christmas still about two weeks away. On Tuesdays Raven got up, played the piano and a little guitar, and then went to work; but, today she got distracted. While taking a break to refill her coffee cup, something outside the kitchen window caught her attention.

There, right in clear vision, was a raven playing in the snow. It was stopping every few flips and slides to look right in her direction as if beckoning her to join him. Without hesitation, Raven was on the move. Choosing to exit out the lakeside patio doors, Raven set off to get a better view of her new friend. She didn't have to go far, for the sizeable black bird had followed her around the house, watching her through the windows. It now continued its antics about three feet from the edge of the cozy stone patio.

Wrapping herself in a blanket, Raven sat in the comfortable hand-crafted wooden chair to the left of the fire pit. From her chosen seat, she could easily see the joyful snow dance and far out across the frozen lake. No matter how many times she sat here, it still took her breath away.

Once again, the comical black bird took a flying leap and dove into the snow before rolling over several times, taking advantage of the slight decline towards the lake. Once satisfied with his stunt, he jumped straight up, shaking his head. Giggling to herself, Raven wondered if that was to get the snow off its head or to get his bearings. To her delight, the little guy bulldozed his way back up with his beak cutting playfully through the snow and started all over again. It was a delightful slice of time and Raven relished it.

She had always loved ravens. How could she not? But when she discovered that not many people had these types of experiences with ravens and definitely not on a regular basis, she grew to respect the intimate interludes even more.

She had made this discovery when she first submitted her *Kissed* project for approval in a commercial music business class. When the idea of Raven becoming the costumed character *Ravyn* was introduced, of course there was much discussion and digression about ravens. Many people in the class shared that they had never even seen a raven and probably wouldn't know about the bird if Edgar Allen Poe hadn't made the intriguing raven so famous. That comment had many people joining in the woeful chorus of high school memories where they had to memorize and recite the infamous poem.

Raven, on the other hand, had seen ravens all of her life. She had just assumed it was that way for everyone. After learning differently, she logically mused, "Well, some people are surrounded by cats, some by dogs, and me by ravens."

Some would argue that ravens flocked around her just because of her name, but according to Raven's mother, that was not an accurate tale. Lydia had on many occasions told the story of Raven's naming, but Raven wasn't really sure how much of it to believe. The older she got, the longer the story became, until Raven had trouble remembering the details of the earliest version. The story was generally prompted by someone exclaiming in disbelief, "Is that a raven?!"

Even now, because Raven had heard the story so many times, she could hear her mother's voice reciting a version of it in her head:

"Almost immediately following the childbirth, the midwife asked me if we had chosen a name. We had been thinking about Marjory; but then I looked out the window and there sat the raven. You know that raven showed up the night we learned we were pregnant and kept me company so many nights thereafter. So, she's our little Raven!" The crowd would applaud and guffaw at the story, shaking their heads in wonderment, smiling at the little girl. Humorously, as a child, all Raven could truly appreciate about that story was that she hadn't been named Marjory.

Raven watched the acrobatic show until she could no longer resist the invitation. Being careful not to invade her little friend's space, she jumped in the snow and made snow angels until her arms and legs felt frozen.

A quick coffee warmup and change of clothes later found Raven ready for her shift. She was exhilarated. Not ready to say goodbye to her little feathered friend just yet she decided to walk to work that day. She talked to him as she headed down the trail towards Denny's. As hoped, he came along running and playing in her wake; but, after five minutes of a slight incline and completely silly conversation, they parted ways. The raven took a great flying leap into a little tuft of snow. A couple of flips later had him rolling down the hill they had just climbed with absolute glee. Raven's last sight of him included tail feathers wiggling into a snowbank and nothing else.

Giggling out loud, Raven returned to her path. She was early today, so continued on slowly, lifting her chin to enjoy the warm sun shining on her exposed face, the snow crunching deliciously beneath her feet. It was quiet. Of course, it wasn't long before the thoughts in her head began to cause a bit of noise.

A lot had happened to Raven in a short period of time. Some of it she was still processing. The land deal had been signed on Monday, as expected, with a confident Dreyfus walking her through the proceedings. Raven hadn't worried too much about Denny's response. The idea was just what he had described to Raven so many years ago. He dreamed of owning a cabin campground, family atmosphere, surrounded by music and the arts, with both live professional performances and summer camps.

Raven guessed the latter part came from the fact that he was so good with kids, but had never had any of his own. And Raven, well the interesting circumstances presented an opportunity to watch, with great satisfaction, as others got the chance to explore their dreams. Hers had been handed to her so easily, and then taken away in such a devastating manner; and yet, here she was, the happiest and feeling more at peace than she could ever remember.

Life was funny. Where would she be right now if *that* hadn't happened? Would she be this happy? How would every one's life around her be different if she had spent the last nine years on the road with *Kissed?*

Humoring herself with her own vision of Christmas pasts she saw possibilities that included being so wrapped up in work that she only emailed friends a belated holiday wish, running from show to show, surrounded by the materialism of music, being a prisoner of her own life. And of course, seems like there is always a Richard or an Argus around trying to use you for their own personal gain.

Maybe it was her fault, a question that never failed to circle around when Richard entered her thoughts. Maybe her behavior caused him to go mad in some strange, slow way. The funny thing is, it didn't matter anymore. No more questions. No more blame. The lightbulb finally went bright. Perhaps an impatient angel had heard enough of her prayers and said, *"enough already,"* poofing the idea into her head. For on this day Raven recognized that she had forgiven not only herself, but everyone else involved. It was the most beautiful feeling of freedom she ever remembered. She wasn't perfect, and didn't have to be.

She was God's creation, His child, as He made her. The journey she had taken had led her right here, to this wonderful place. The mistakes she had made, the tragedies experienced, her life lessons were a pathway of realization.

Her visions included how she was given her dreams on a platter and materialism had become important. Then she had been stripped of everything, including her dignity; and, while she prayed to Him throughout the journey, she didn't give herself to Him completely . . . until now. This is why she never got married. This is why she was already complete. She could love her friends and her family, but she belonged to Him. Her gift of music was her mate, and her only job was to be the best she could be at every given moment out of respect and love for Him.

Feeling as if an incredible burden had been lifted from her shoulders, she heard Wally in her head saying, "Yep, don't matter where you been, what are you doing right now?"

Immersed in her own thoughts of joy as she was skipping down the road, because well, that's what Wally would do. She didn't notice the dark-eyed beauty in a scarf and hat perfectly tailored to match her green eyes.

"Raven?" a tentative voice interrupted.

"Jasmine!" shouted Raven, as she ran the rest of the way to greet her long-lost friend. As she threw her arms around her in a hug, she was struck by the momentary realization that yesterday she might not have shown the same mercy or grace. *Life is good.*

CHAPTER TWENTY-TWO

Jasmine sat at the bar, entertained by Wally with Raven dropping into the conversation between customers. Wally was consciously focusing the conversation on their school time together. He didn't, after all, want to be the first to address the elephant in the room.

Denny came in some time later. He had been out chopping wood. Until April when the building project was to begin, this was how he cleared the property. He cut down one tree at a time when he had the need, and only when he had the need. Walking past with his arms full of logs to put by the fire, he stopped dead when he saw Jasmine, a couple of logs rolling off the stack onto the floor. Seeing Raven's smile, he dropped the rest of the logs and yelled a boisterous welcome with outstretched arms.

"Jasmine! Welcome to Denny's Den," completing his welcome with a big bear hug. And before Denny could even realize, the two young gentlemen, Alexander and Charles, who owned and ran the coffee shop in the center of town, had picked the logs up off the wooden floor and put them in their rightful place.

Hours later finally had Jasmine and Raven sitting alone in the quiet little corner Raven loved so much, the same one she had been standing in waiting for her Denny's Den debut performance. All conversation about triviality had long passed and Jasmine finally started the conversation that Raven knew she was trying to work up the courage to start all day.

"Raven, I have to ask you something, and if you don't want to talk about it, I understand," started a tentative Jasmine, but Raven could tell this wasn't the same naïve little girl you could push around. Her experiences on the road had hardened her, robbed her of her innocent trust in people.

Sad, Raven thought for both her and Jasmine. *In those days, her innocence irritated me and now if only I could give it back to her, I would.*

"When all of that went down, did you plan to leave us and go solo?" Jasmine's voice trembled with her eyes teetering between loyal disbelief and accusatory betrayal.

"Jasmine, the reason you are asking me, and the reason you are so upset, is because you know that isn't true. You know I wouldn't have done that without talking to you and Kat. I'm not so sure about Python, but then she would have just rejoiced anyway, as I'm sure she did."

Jasmine raised her eyebrows and nodded her head in agreement, confirming what Raven had imagined; but, it didn't matter anymore. She hoped Python achieved what she needed.

"That's what Angela said," Jasmine replied. "She's something else, isn't she? She wouldn't let me quit. I went to her after the apology video. She said she didn't think the solo stuff was true and of course that made me more upset, I mean we just left you there!" Her eyes growing wider in despair at the thought of what she had done.

"She told me that if I was quitting for you, that that wouldn't make you happy. And then she said if I didn't believe her, I should come ask you. She actually dared me!" laughed Jasmine through her tears. "She reminds me of you, you know, so strong," Jasmine's voice trailed off, thoughts still swimming inside her head.

"Why would they do that? Try to split us up like that? They had documents RayRay," an endearing nickname Raven had completely forgotten about, her heart swelling with joy at hearing it again.

"Seriously. They had contracts, prepared press releases, album cover, the works. *Ravyn Flies Solo, Ravyn Spreads Her Wings*, something like that. Python went in full force when she heard that," finished Jasmine, shaking her head, trying to sort out the fuzzy details.

"I don't know, Jasmine. I was presented with the same plan on my end, with a few additional clauses," said Raven flatly. "I refused," she added with a light-hearted shrug.

"It was him, wasn't it? That hurt you? Oh my God, is *that* why he hurt you?" gasped Jasmine, finally connecting some of the dots, obviously fighting tears.

"I didn't know. I couldn't even look at you in the hospital. They told us you got caught in the fire with Richard. And then I saw the video and, oh my God. Raven, what did he do to you?"

"Ssssshh, sshhh. Stop Jasmine, it's okay. Stop!" demanded Raven. "It was a long time ago and he's gone. Seriously, it's okay. We're good, aren't we?"

"Okay, here is the deal," Raven said, changing her tone, trying to add levity to the situation. "I only have three rules you have to comply with in order for us to truly rekindle our friendship, and I really hope we do. First is, we don't cry over him anymore. Not ever. Not a tear. Hear me?" Jasmine, quickly wiping the now streaming tears, nodded.

"Second, we don't talk about that event. Ever. It's over. It's done. It no longer has the power to hurt us unless we let it," Jasmine nodded, smiling. Raven had always made her feel so strong, so capable.

"And third, don't touch the hair," Raven winked, motioning and sounding like a diva, making Jasmine laugh. That last rule was a double-edged punchline. Obviously, Raven's personal space was important to her, but that also happened to be the same thing Python always demanded of makeup artists attaching her final costume adornment, the eye mask.

To Raven's dismay, Jasmine couldn't stay longer than one day. She was going to spend the night at the hotel and be up for an early flight, but she promised to be back. Raven even mentioned the Fan Club party that was still looming ahead, suggesting they could drive up together and really give the fans a run for their money. Jasmine promised to look at her calendar and try to work it out. With a final hug, Jasmine jumped in her fancy rental car and blew a kiss out the window as she began her short journey back to town.

CHAPTER TWENTY-THREE

That week at the bar was much easier. Some high school girls that Michael knew jumped at the chance to work at the place that had the whole town buzzing with excitement. And Mario's nephew, Prego, who had just arrived for the holidays and planned to stay until the wind blew him in a different direction, applied for the bar back job. Having the instincts that he did, Denny hired him on the spot.

The waitresses were a little harder. After narrowing down the candidates and excluding the girls that were there out of love or obsession for Raven or Michael, three were left. He asked Raven to decide, so she hired all three and started taking Friday's shift off to help Michael prepare for the evening's video shoot. She told Denny what she had done before giggling and running out of the office, never giving him a chance to respond. He didn't care. He was blessed. Thank *you, Lord. Life is good.*

That week Raven was also communicating with the Fan Club President, Magicmusic21, to finalize the party arrangements. The conversations moved from email to Skype calls. His voice was pleasant, but with a thick Boston accent. No matter how raucous the vowels sounded, the Boston speech pattern had always seemed to mesmerize her. As a singer that focused on vowel structure, she had never quite understood how to shape her mouth to fake a Boston accent. She could sooner convince someone she was from England than from Boston. And she wasn't the only one. The very first time Musicmagic21 and Raven shared a voice conversation, Raven couldn't help but be reminded of an ongoing joke that had been playing out almost since Raven's arrival.

It started with Jacob sitting at the bar looking at the menu, which Raven now knew was a silly ritual. If Fred had eyes, like he had ears, he could easily begin making the barbeque special of the day upon seeing Jacob's truck coming down the dirt road and pulling into the gravel lot.

While Fred's eyes were not capable of that feat, his ears were something special. You could whisper a mile away and Fred would be happy to yell back an answer for you. Raven secretly believed that Fred's hearing skills were continuing to develop so he could be entertained by their shenanigans while he was cooking in the kitchen. Either that or he was cooking more quietly.

On this day Wally had decided he was from Boston and was talking to Jacob about some fancy mechanical part Jacob needed to finish the BMW sitting down in his shop. Wally, who was brilliant in many areas, had a severe disinterest in how machines worked. He wanted to push a button and be done with it, so much so that a battery-operated pencil sharpener that began working slow would have him swearing the thing up and down and giving it a famous "Fonzie" tap, although without the television character's finesse.

Fred was used to these events. He would get up from where he was reading or stop watering the plants, walk over to the junk drawer in the kitchen and return with batteries that he would drop ceremoniously into Wally's lap. Wally's self-pointed laughter, of course, amusing him further.

On this memorable day, you could hear Fred laughing from the kitchen. It started with just a short outburst, but they seemed to grow in both length and mirth. You see, despite Wally's distaste for machines, he could take any dialogue and turn it into an acting exercise. In this case, he was trying to master the Boston accent while working with unfamiliar automotive terms and Jacob was as patient as a parent trying to teach a two-year-old how to say *Dada*.

Finally, Fred stuck his head out of the pass-through and you could see small tears of laughter trying to spill their way down his face. Fred, dressed in his usual blue flannel, loved machines. So, hearing his beloved carrying on this conversation in an accent he hadn't quite mastered had struck the giggle button.

"My man, I don't think I have ever said this to you. But THAT dialect needs a little bit of work," Fred stated, barely getting the words out before busting into laughter again. No doubt his personal perception included the image of Wally standing over the motor trying to fix it by hitting it with a bat. A silly as that was, it might not have been too far off-base.

Musicmagic21, however, had spent most of his life in Boston, details he freely offered even though he had not been asked, and Raven wondered if she could get the two of them together so Wally could really hear the accent in action. As it turned out, Raven was going to get her chance to make the introduction. The Fan Club party had been scheduled for the following Thursday, December 23rd.

Musicmagic21 said his friends of old called him *Magic*, explaining he had been fascinated with magic tricks as a kid and still tinkered with illusions when he could; but, most new people he met called him *Boston*. Raven laughed, saying she understood why "Boston" had stuck. The man continued sharing that he had made arrangements at the Grand Teton's Resort. Raven provided a list of people she wanted to attend. She had already been informed by Denny that even if he had to close the bar, she was not re-entering that phase of her life without backup.

As the conversations ensued, Raven was surprised at his knowledge of *Kissed* history, despite the fact that he was the Fan Club President. Their last phone meeting had them laughing over a backstage event, leading Raven to ask if they had ever met. She only remembered a few people being present during that bit of chaos, but it was such a long time ago and, like Jasmine, the details had become fuzzy.

"Not that night. The Fan Club was set up in the second green room. We were supposed to have a meet and greet, but Python had all of you screaming and running in different directions. I came out to see how much longer and well, I kinda witnessed it from behind a curtain. Sorry about that. But we have actually met on several occasions. Who knows, maybe you will recognize me," the man laughed with sarcasm and maybe just a little bit of . . . was it hope?

Not receiving any response, for Raven didn't know what to say, the man returned the conversation to finalizing the event details. He asked if Raven could arrive a few hours early for some photographs and some face-to-face interviews with fans. This didn't thrill Raven, but she knew it was part of the game. It wasn't that she didn't enjoy talking about music with others. It was just that *Ravyn* was so far removed from her current life that she couldn't help feeling a bit like a fraud. Recognizing these thoughts were completely ridiculous considering the truth that had set these proceedings in motion, she agreed without complaint. As Raven expected, they were also hoping she would perform a few songs.

And finally, he mentioned with a bit of hesitation, that the other members of *Kissed*, including Elizabeth Tonkem, had requested an invitation. He asked Raven if she wanted to accept or deny that request. Preferring not to see the other two previous band mates without a private visit first, she hesitated, imagining the headlines that would be printed and blogged about her lack of congeniality if she said "No." So, she again agreed, already wishing the event was over.

Deciding to focus on the glass half-full perspective, Raven was quite happy that it would be over and done before Christmas, not looming ahead casting a shadow on the holiday festivities. On Christmas Eve, she would be free to start a new phase of her life where the past was really behind, and the future ahead, an exciting new beginning.

CHAPTER TWENTY-FOUR

Semantics. Details. Raven sighed as she worked to add all the new information into her Smart Device calendar, slightly irritated at herself. The chore wasn't difficult. She was irritated because for a very brief unnerving moment caught herself thinking about how helpful Richard had been. *She needed an assistant, but how could she ever trust anyone with that position again?*

Between her work at the bar, the details involving her identity release, the upcoming build project to begin in April, the long-term web clients she continued to serve, helping Michael, and finally, the need to write that promised album. She had gone from a simple quiet life to one of absolute schedule chaos.

She hadn't promised anyone an album release specifically, but Raven and Dreyfus had discussed this thoroughly. While Bear Crossing was at this moment debt free, it would take some doing for everything to get in place and a profit to be turned. Raven needed to have a new album on the shelves by April; and, despite her stated position that she would never work with Diamond Back Records again, she couldn't quite get Angela's offer out of her head.

Regardless of the increased workload at the bar and everyone having additional responsibilities on their plate for Bear Crossing, that week passed in the blink of an eye and also like clockwork. The changes instituted at Denny's Den had worked themselves into a rhythm and everyone was back to their regular comedic routine during shifts.

Denny had given Raven the day off on Thursday, the day of the Fan Club party, and had decided to close the bar at the end of regular food service so they all could attend the event. Everyone had received their formal invitations and left the bar excited to put on their best threads. Well, perhaps that was only true of Wally. Anna and Michael were also coming. They were all driving up together in Marna's delivery van, assuming Denny could figure out how to put the seats back in.

Jasmine was coming in with the rest of *Kissed*. No doubt Python had arranged some sort of grand entrance. This thought was funny to Raven. In essence, the party was for her; and, while she doubted she could achieve it, would prefer to sneak in than stand in a spotlight. Even after all these years, she knew that was not true for Python.

Looking in the mirror one more time at her reflection, she shrugged and said what Jessie always said to the mirror upon final inspection of an outfit, "That'll do, little pig. That'll do."

Turning away and giggling at the memory, inspired most likely by their hour-long phone conversation that morning, Raven grabbed the sticky note where she had jotted down Jessie's flight information and entered it into her calendar, forwarding it to Denny who had insisted on picking her up days before. Jessie couldn't come today, but would arrive before the Christmas Eve gathering tomorrow evening. She was going to stay until the first of the year. This news had them both giggling and making plans just like they were planning one of their infamous sleepovers in high school.

Finished with her task, Raven tossed the note into the garbage, grabbed her things, and jumped in the little yellow beetle bug car that suited her so well. Ten minutes or so later, she was walking into Marna's flower shop only to find it empty. Marna's laughter led Raven out the open back door where Denny was trying to figure out the van seats. Marna had taken them out the very first day and they had collected dust in storage ever since. Upon focusing her vision on the action, Raven could understand why Marna was enjoying it so much. Denny, was speaking confident phrases like, "Oh, I see. I got it now!" but had never looked as clumsy or ungraceful as that moment.

Marna, seeing Raven, produced a slow, steady whistle. While Raven was dressed in a simple flowing pantsuit, all black with a simple ruffle running down the front, Marna found her absolutely stunning. Denny, having finally managed to get the first seat in place, turned and repeated Marna's whistle.

"Stop it, I couldn't look any plainer," said a slightly embarrassed Raven, but they didn't have time to respond beyond their disagreeing shaking heads as a blaring car horn indicated the arrival of her ride. Kissing them quickly on the cheek and shouting "Love you both! See you in a couple of hours," Raven left them staring after her as she sprinted through the flower shop and into the limo waiting out front.

Still a little flushed, Raven blurted "Hi!" to the driver as she settled into her seat behind him.

Upon seeing her strap her seatbelt into place, the driver, who seemed a little nervous, never quite made direct eye contact in the rear-view mirror stammered, "All, all set Miss Reynolds?"

As they entered the highway that would take them about thirty miles north, the driver introduced himself as Luke and invited her to have some champagne, compliments, of course, of the *Kissed* Fan Club. Seeing the chilling bottle of one of her old favorites, she assumed it must have been printed somewhere on a fan page and catalogued into the mind of the club's trusty President.

Accepting the invitation and filling the rather large crystal flute, she took a sip and allowed the taste to envelope her. It was just as she remembered, but she couldn't have too much. Champagne gave her the giggles and she wanted to have her wits about her.

Luke, swerving a bit abruptly to avoid a pot hole, startled Raven to the point that her glass tipped and the rest of the clear bubbling liquid dumped itself into the ice bucket. Chuckling inwardly, she realized she couldn't have done that again if she tried. Seeing that as some kind of sign, she replaced the crystal glass where she had found it. She didn't need any more to relax, she thought, taking deep breaths. Closing her eyes and settling back into the comfortable seat, she listened to the music and wondered how the night's memory would be imprinted in her scrapbook of life.

So relaxed, thought Raven. *Why am I so sleepy? So sleepy.* As she drifted off to sleep she realized she was listening to Tchaikovsky's Symphony no. 6, *Pathetique*.

As the car came to a stop, Raven was in a state of disorientation. The driver's car door slamming caught her attention and she heard voices outside in what sounded to be a heated conversation. She felt the rush of the cold wind enter the cabin as the driver finally opened her door and stood back to allow her exit. Trying to remember where she was, she fumbled with the seatbelt unsuccessfully. A man then reached in and said with a Boston accent, "Let me help you, Miss Reynolds," offering his hand to help her step from the car after releasing her from the restraints.

Boston. Magic. Fan Club. Words such as this were bouncing around Raven's mind as she was being escorted up some steep stone steps, each gentleman supporting an elbow. Despite her confusion, or maybe because of it, Raven began counting steps and noticing direction turns. It was a technique she had learned to conquer fear or confusion in any one location. Count your steps, observe your surroundings, sit facing the door, etc. The technique had worked so well that it was something Raven did in her subconscious in every new place, this one being no exception.

Once inside the front door, they went fifteen steps straight down the hall, turned left, and then down a single flight of stairs before exiting right into a rather small room. The room, like many in this part of the country, was rustic in nature with dark wooden beams and a light neutral color splashed in between. There were also two window wells. Of course, this time of year, their greenhouse-shaped tops were completely buried in snow.

The gentlemen led her to a rather large wingback chair in the back of the room; and, with a bit of firmness, sat her down. Once she was seated, her observation opportunity was limited. The lights from the lighting rig were already turned on and shining directly in her eyes. Not to mention that she was also still very confused, as if she was on the outside of her body looking in. *What was wrong with her?*

Closing her eyes to relieve the pulsations caused by the lights, she took several deep breaths, each breath seeming to bring back more clarity. Hearing voices in the distance, she decided to take a play from Fred's playbook and listened closely. The two men were talking just outside the door at the bottom of the stairwell. The driver was leaving. Everything was right on schedule. It wasn't until Raven heard the Boston accent, whom she assumed was Musicmagic21 say, "Stick to the plan," that her radar went into full force. She may have been confounded, but her internal red radar flag began waving clearly. *Pay attention, Raven!*

Still seeing double, but beginning to gain her bearings, Raven peered in the direction of the man with the Boston accent who returned to a position behind the camera and lighting lamps.

"Raven, may I call you Raven?" the man's voice said from behind the spots in Raven's eyes.

"And you are?" Raven managed politely, not answering his question.

"I'm so sorry, I'm Boston of course. Thank you for agreeing to this interview. Are you feeling better now? You were white as a sheet when you arrived," he said. Not giving Raven a true window for response he continued, "So let's get started. Shall we? Busy night!"

Despite the fact that she was taken aback by the man's behavior, her fair certainty that something had been in the champagne, and the internal voice telling her to run, Raven couldn't move. She could think about it, but her body was not answering her brain's commands. She was getting her sight back and the fogginess that had enveloped her was lifting, but she still felt like she was having an out-of-body experience. She would have to wait. After all, hadn't she learned on a previous occasion that a well-thought-out plan was better than a rash and panicked decision? Plus, was it possible she was just nervous and had over-reacted?

The next hour actually proved to be more relaxing. Boston was asking questions about how the girls had met and some of the funny stories that had persisted all these years, even though Elizabeth Tonkem would have had no memory of them. It all seemed pretty harmless, so Raven continued to internally question her earlier panic attack.

And then, of course, came the topic of Richard.

She hadn't really thought about how she would handle him in the interview. With the focus being on current events and the thought of facing Python for the first time before cameras, she had completely forgotten that no one knew what had happened to her. His name was not tarnished. As far as the world was concerned, he was a talented man that had tragically lost his life in a fire. *Idiotic oversight*. The man was dead. Had she publicized what had happened, her life would have been a completely different kind of media circus.

"Do you miss him?" the thick Boston accent asked, interrupting her thoughts.

And before she could stop herself said, "Sometimes," reminded of her own thoughts the previous morning. The admittance produced a sick feeling in the pit of her stomach, but it was true. When Richard hadn't been in one of his love manic phases, she had quite enjoyed his friendship.

Raven didn't realize how long the silence dragged on, lost in her own thoughts; and, then came the most surprising question thus far.

"Could you ever forgive him?"

Tired of the current game and not liking the way this interview was going, Raven said, "It appears your camera crew is late, or perhaps you need a bigger budget? Regardless, this is a stationary shot. I believe now that the camera is rolling, you can come join me here. Although you might want to turn down the lights a tad."

"Would that make you more comfortable?" came the sounds of Boston from behind the camera.

"Well it would certainly feel more like an interview and less of an interrogation. What time is it? Shouldn't we be joining the party upstairs?" she asked, wondering if a simple nudge would get them out the door.

Raven had two objectives for making this man sit in the chair beside her. First, it got him away from the door. While she didn't have straight access, the odds were better if she needed it. Even if just to make a diva exit as Python would have done after question number one in those conditions. Second, Raven wanted to look this man in the eyes so she could understand the motivation behind his questions. Something didn't feel right. She had agreed to tell her story, but she wanted to be in control. She wasn't going to instantly trust some guy who had followed the band around like a sophisticated stalker for fifteen years.

Sitting down in the wing-back chair opposite Raven, after making the lights more agreeable, he apologized for her perception of his tactics and admitted that he was actually kind of new at this. Raven observed the man closely. He was quite tall and had long hair, all one length, that resembled the shade of coal. He was dressed in a tuxedo and smelled of an old cologne she used to love. *What was that?* Searching her mind, she couldn't quite find the name.

"So, you didn't answer my question," stated the man next to her in a softer voice than before.

"And you didn't answer mine," returned Raven. "Pardon my bluntness; but, for someone who was so direct on the phone, as well as behind the camera when I was in the spotlight, you seem to be avoiding eye contact with me. Shouldn't we be leaving?" she asked again, moving to check her cell phone.

"Raven, there you go, spoiling all the fun. Don't bother," the man said, a little too familiar. Looking into Raven's gaze for the first time as she pulled her hand from the bag holding the phone, he continued without any accent at all, "It won't work."

Look in the eyes people. Look in the eyes. Isn't that what his headline had read? She was indeed now looking in his eyes, and there he was . . . a dead man staring back at her.

CHAPTER TWENTY-FIVE

The Grand Teton Ballroom was decorated brilliantly. First, as you walked in, your gaze set upon snow-covered mountains through large picture windows set in small sitting alcoves. The alcoves themselves consisted of comfy little bench seats with throw pillows and a little ledge along the back that was perfect for sitting your elbow or your drink. They were just as comfy as they looked, a server shared as he invited Wally to check it out.

"When no events are planned, I come down here and curl up with a book or my mp3 player a lot of days. I have to set my phone alarm in case I fall asleep!" shared the young waiter who had no name tag.

Wally did indeed check out the alcoves and what started as a mild curiosity soon turned into a major photoshoot with Raven's crazy kin all climbing in separately, together, and finally all at once just for fun, including Michael. Denny climbed out of the booth laughing.

"We have now made Raven proud and have photographs to prove it," he grinned at Michael who did indeed get some great shots for his blog and the Bear Crossing scrapbook, along with the last one taken by the server who had observed the entire event with glee.

"Speaking of Raven, when does she get here?" asked Fred, looking around the group for an answer. Everyone responded with they thought she would already be there. The fact that he didn't know instantly had Denny reaching for his cell phone and texting his Goddaughter for confirmation. He knew that if she was in the middle of an interview her cell phone would be turned off, but you never know.

Around the outside of the room there were many little white lights that looked like stationary snowflakes on top of the dark wooden panels. In the corner sat a medium-size triangle stage surrounded in luxurious draping, requiring two steps up to arrive on the platform. Currently there were two images teetering on the screen at the back of the stage. The original faces album cover, and a similar concept done after Raven's departure, where all members had received a costume makeover to help with the original member charade. The picture window alcoves were spread out on either side of the stage, with a marble dance floor surrounded by round tables in cream-colored linen cloths.

In addition to stations around the room, there were also some exhibits out in the front room where the bar was located. Each exhibit station was able to play multiple videos from the *Kissed* vaults. Some people had already started putting them to good use as they were waiting for the event to begin.

A few minutes later, a man with a heavy Boston accent got on stage and welcomed everyone through the microphone.

"Hello everyone. I am known in this setting as Musicmagic21, President of the *Kissed Fan Club*. Some of my friends call me Magic, because I like to do magic tricks," he paused dramatically. "No one? Okay, well in that case, most people call me Boston," he said, laying the accent on as thick as he could towards the end. He was smooth and knew exactly how to handle an impatient, anxious crowd.

"We are still waiting for some of our ladies to arrive, but while we do, feel free to enjoy the slide show that is about to begin or watch your favorite videos around the outside of the room and at the bar. There are plenty of appetizers and beverages, so make yourself at home! We will bring out the guests of honor as soon as they are done powdering their noses."

Another big laugh from the audience had the man gliding off the stage and immediately out the door into the staffing area. Denny repeatedly checked his phone that remained in the palm of his hand. Five more minutes he said to himself, scanning the crowd for Angela.

He wasn't sure what he would do, but he would risk being called the over-protective Godfather and find out what was going on. Preoccupied momentarily by the slideshow sharing pictures from the very first *Kissed* tour, Denny mused over how he liked the live shots better than the photo sessions. Raven was never more alive than when she was on stage, and posing for pictures always appeared just a little stiff.

Not able to turn his eyes away from the entertainment, he watched two tours' worth before checking his phone again and actively going to look for Angela. Why Angela? Because she was a woman that got things done, and fast.

Wally and Fred were dancing to the music accompanying the slideshow, enjoying the rare night off. They were standing in earshot of Boston who had returned and was giving orders to the staff, also engaging in short conversations with the people around him.

"You know, Wally, I think I owe you an apology," said Fred sheepishly. "I hate to give up the joke because it gets funnier every time, but that guy from Boston talks just like you, so you're better than I thought!"

Wally held him just a little tighter as they continued to sway and move to the music. Wally had actually been listening attentively to Boston. He had even orchestrated where they were dancing so he could eavesdrop. Not often did he have the opportunity to listen to a Boston accent live and in person. But there was something strange about the conversations Boston was having with the people he passed. Wally couldn't put his finger on it. There was something so familiar, but Fred, pointing and laughing at Raven singing into the camera with her eyes crossed for fun through her eye mask, distracted Wally, making him forget about the strange déja vu.

Just about that time Fred said, "You know, it's getting late and we have gone through four slideshows of tours. Aren't the girls supposed to be here for this?" They both turned to go look for the others without a second of hesitation.

Denny found Angela just as Fred and Wally found Denny. Angela was leading in the four ladies currently working as the band *Kissed*.

"Denny!" said Jasmine, running to hug him as Kat lifted her hand in a wave and said, "Hey DenDen!" while Python provided a simple nod of acknowledgement.

"Where's Raven?" asked Jasmine as she stepped back from the bear hugs she had been missing for nine years.

"What do you mean? I thought she was with you? Angela?" asked Denny, a slight hint of panic in his voice. "She came here earlier to meet Boston for an interview. We expected her to be waiting for us when we arrived."

Immediately Angela took action. She walked into the main event room and returned to the little bar area with Boston. Denny smirked as he imagined her pulling him out of there by his earlobe.

"Where's Raven," demanded Angela. They were starting to draw a little crowd out in the makeshift event bar as Anna and Michael joined the group. Angela obviously wasn't fazed one bit about disrupting the event proceedings.

"I don't know," answered Boston. "We finished early, she got a phone call, said she wanted some fresh air. I don't know. Is she prone to talk to someone named Jessie for say almost two hours?" It was a statement that actually had the Bear Crossing group chuckling. Even Michael knew that a phone call with Jessie could easily go on for hours if time allowed.

"Something's not right. She wouldn't do this," said Marna. "Maybe she fell. Those shoes she was wearing were incredible, but looked dangerous. You remember Denny, when the driver picked her up at the flower shop today? We should begin a search."

Everyone quickly shifted to move as Angela instructed her staff to get the hotel manager to begin a search, but Jasmine said, "Stop!" halting further movement. All eyes turned towards her immediately, except Angela who motioned for her staff to act on her original request.

"What did you say about a flower shop?" asked Jasmine.

"What do you mean? Raven dropped her car off at my shop today because she is riding home with us. Her car will be waiting there for her. She looked stunning. Come to think of it though, she sprinted through that shop like she had on sneakers," said Marna, rambling nervously without realizing before asking, "Why?"

"What time did the driver pick her up?" Jasmine said in a monotone voice, turning red.

"Four o'clock. What's going on Jasmine?" interjected a demanding Denny with Fred and Wally peering over his shoulder like the demand had a punch to the third power.

Slowly Jasmine was turning to Python. "I heard Python on the phone today, saying something about a flower shop at 4:00 and did he have the address. Where's Raven, Python?"

"I don't know what you are talking about, Jasmine. Shut your trap!" spit an angry Python.

"Who were you talking to Python? Why were you discussing Raven's limousine schedule? I would have thought assisting with her travel arrangements would be far beneath *you*," demanded Angela, her tone meaning business.

"I was talking to Boston. That limo picked us up next and we were just confirming," Python shrieked nervously.

All eyes turned to Boston for confirmation. Boston stuttered at first but then did confirm and began offering the explanation that he had misspoke and said the wrong time, and Python was just reminding him that the flower shop was first. Wally was watching him closely, curiously.

Angela looked at Boston with one eye closed, scrutinizing him thoroughly. Turning to the little crowd that had gathered Angela asked, "Has anyone here ever seen this man before today? Speak up. Anyone?"

There was silence in the room, with the exception of the resort manager busting through the crowd to report that the grounds were being searched at that very moment. Angela thanked him for the speedy response.

"I think we also need to call the police, please tell them to hurry," added Angela.

"The police?" shouted Boston, "Whoa. Whoa. Wait a minute."

Wally was the first to notice the man had spoken in fear without a lick of accent. He simultaneously recognized the most recent stuttered response and pattern of speech he had used inside was an acting improv technique, one used by false psychics all the time . . . ask the question, then give the answer. Without further ado, he exclaimed loudly, "You're an actor!"

Angela confirmed with the manager that she did indeed want the police called and then turned back to the man they had all been calling Boston, but now seemed to have no discernable Boston accent.

"Talk," demanded Angela.

"I'm an actor. Call my agency. I was hired to come here and bide time while the beautiful Miss Raven Reynolds eloped. Her family, here, they don't like the man. They were to make their getaway while everyone was occupied at this event. I'm sure she is safe. The guy that hired me was obviously in love," stammered the actor who was beginning to crumble under pressure.

This statement had more than one person about to defy that theory loudly when Angela put up her hand to silence them, a command no one could resist following.

"Do you know where she is now?" fired off Angela quickly, real concern beginning to show in her eyes.

When the actor shook his head, Angela returned her gaze to Python who had begun to back to the outskirts of the room.

"Get back here, Python!" Angela demanded, stomping her foot and pointing to a place on the floor in front of her.

Enough people had been listening long enough that whether Python was planning on complying or not made no difference. The circle around the room pushed her back into the center, to the exact point where Angela was pointing.

"You know something, and I want to know what it is."

Python didn't answer her query, only shook her head with real fear starting to creep into her eyes as Angela leaned in and up on her toes, only about an inch separating their noses. Despite the height difference, Angela stared her down, completely in control.

"I told you when that file came across my desk that I suspected you had more knowledge than you shared, but I would not dig if you didn't give me a reason to. This, my dear one, is a reason. Now talk."

Although Angela had kept her voice low, the people that mattered to Raven overheard enough.

"What?!" exclaimed both Kat and Jasmine. The Bear Crossing crew was also looking at each other, whispering, trying to confirm what they heard.

"Not now," Angela looked at them sharply. "Get her phone."

Denny, admiring this woman as much as he did and not disappointed one bit this evening, let her work the turf. At this brilliant request, Denny stepped forward and grabbed Python's hands, holding them behind her back. He was doing his best not to lose his cool, no matter how much he wanted to strangle her. Denny didn't really care that he didn't have all the facts. His gut was pointing right at Python as an evil doer.

Taking the retrieved cell phone from Jasmine, Angela demanded the privacy lock code. But in that moment Angela noted the last message that had come in, still sitting on top of the screen that read only three words: the name "Argus" followed by the message "drop-off complete."

"Argus! I should have known. You are a stupid, stupid woman Python. Raven returning would have made you millions. Where is she?" demanded Angela again. "Python, if I learn that you know something and you didn't step up to the plate, I will make sure you never, ever work in the music business again. Your name will be MUD," exclaimed Angela, knowing exactly how to hit Python where it hurt.

With Angela's gaze still never flinching, and hearing sirens in the distance, Python glared at Angela and cried, "He was blackmailing me!"

Seeing her technique was working. Angela said strongly, "We will deal with whatever that is later, give me an address!" Seeing Python hesitate, the stout woman demanded, "Now, Python. Give me the address."

At Python's direction, Angela started scrolling through the text messages, telling the others to get their cell phones out at the same time. As she searched, she spouted off her own phone number and then looked up searching for the young man she had such high hopes for. She found him, holding his mom's hand, both looking completely distressed and helpless.

"Michael, take a picture of this address on her phone. You too, Denny. You guys get going. I'll deal with the police and give them what they need. Go before they hold you up with questioning," Angela commanded, shooing them out the door, knowing if it was her family she wouldn't be standing there waiting for police with an address in hand.

As Fred and Wally dropped their hold on "Boston" and Denny dropped his hold on Python, Angela raised her left hand above her head and snapped her fingers. People on her staff immediately stepped up to resume the guard positions.

CHAPTER TWENTY-SIX

Raven sat for a very long time just staring at Richard with her mouth wide open in shock. The eyes were definitely Richard's, but nothing else looked the same. Surveying the door, she recognized there were just too many tripods to trip over to make a clean exit.

"Well I see your plastic surgeon did a much better job on you than *mine* did on me. Of course, kind of hard to repair bone and skin that has been drilled into, sliced, and burned," said Raven calmly, calculatingly.

"Raven, I'm so sorry. I'm so sorry for my behavior. I know those words probably aren't enough, but I'm better now. You're better now. I'm off the stuff. I don't have the rage anymore. We can go back to the way it was to be, don't you see? And you don't even have to tell anyone it's me. No one will know. And we can be together like we were meant to be. All you have to do is forgive me." stated the strange mouth attached to her worst nightmare's eyes.

"But you were dead. They said you were dead," said Raven, shaking her head, still trying to find a clean foothold path that would put her in a better position in the room. With this question, however, she met his gaze again. She had to know. *They said he was dead.*

"They only found teeth," clarified Richard. "They assumed the fire was so hot that the rest of me burned. The real truth is, you knocked three teeth out with that last kick, and I deserved it." When Raven didn't say anything else, Richard continued.

"Tell me. What can I do? What can I say so that you will let me back in your life? You trusted me once. You said you loved me, that I was family. Can't you give me a second chance?" Richard asked.

The words may have been somewhat pleading, but the delivery was smooth and controlling. They were delivered in a manner that seemed to leave no question of response, like the decisions had already been made and the words were just a required formality. Nothing had changed. Raven knew that the minute she put up a fight, they would be in the same position as before.

"So, no matter what I say, you are going to let me walk out that door? I'm free to leave?" asked Raven directly.

"Weeeell, let's not be so hasty. It's cold out there and I can't let you wander around out there alone at night! That wouldn't be safe. I mean, look at your shoes. Those are not designed for snow and ice. You don't even have a proper coat and have no idea where you are. C'mon, stay here and catch up with me. Give me the chance to prove to you that we should not live our lives apart any longer."

Still sitting like a jack-in-the box ready to pop, Raven studied his face. She had read about things like this where someone came back and the escalation to violence was faster and more destructive if the obsession is not obtained. She had no doubt about whether Richard could be trusted. Without even considering his horrifying past acts, today he had kidnapped her, drugged her, and betrayed her trust yet again by pretending to be someone he wasn't during the arrangements. That kind of premeditation isn't innocent, isn't sincere.

These thoughts were devastating, but important to Raven, who always wanted to believe in the best of people. People did make mistakes and did deserve second chances as life lessons are learned. Raven sat pondering, praying. *What would Jesus do right now?*

"C'mon, you said you missed me sometimes. Aren't you glad to see me?" he asked, taking her left hand and bringing it to his lips.

And there it was, the breaking point. *Don't touch me.* In addition to the physical revulsion, the statement he had said to her so many times during her captivity had flipped a trigger. There was only one other phrase that would have been worse. His favorite as he was sexually abusing her, "Say you are mine." or "You're mine."

Those triggers might have sent her completely off the deep end, but the words he did use were just strong enough to bring forth that wild look in Raven's eye . . . the same witnessed at the bar when Raven awoke covered in doodles. Those six simple words removed all curiosity, all hesitation, and all fear.

Snatching her hand away forcefully, Raven jumped up without warning, grabbed the light tree closest to her, picked it up off the ground and swung it at Richard like a bat. This caught him by surprise, but he hadn't lost all his moves. He did fall out of his chair, doing his best to keep the metal lights on top from colliding with his face, but he reacted faster than Raven had hoped. Grabbing hold of the truss, he shoved it straight towards her, causing her to trip backwards over some cables, falling hard onto her tailbone.

For the next twenty minutes, Raven fought with all her might. Picking up everything and anything she could use for a weapon.

"Didn't have time to bolt everything down, I see," using the memories to fuel her veracity.

The room was now a mess; and, while Raven was holding her own, he was still managing to keep her away from the exit. It was a game to him. Just when she would get close, he would do something that would send her back to the far side of the room. This time he threw her against the original wingback chair that had been assigned to her with such force that it fell backwards. It probably looked more damaging than it was as the chair actually slowed her momentum. As the chair back hit the floor, she rolled and ended on her feet. Raven immediately kicked the chair upright with her left foot and used it as a barricade.

Through it all Richard was talking smoothly, telling her that she would see the light, that they were meant to be together and then he finally did it. "You're mine, Raven. You will always be mine."

That's when Raven saw it, the one item that she had not even noticed in the room. It was like the Heavens opened up and shone a bright light down on the one item in the room that could save her. Had this been a movie, it certainly would have been a cue-celestial-music moment.

The object worthy of such attention was the little table that formerly sat between the two chairs. It had also fallen over with Raven's last forced repositioning, its lace tablecloth no longer concealing its body make-up. As Raven had sat there searching for answers earlier, she didn't even consider it. Perhaps the frilly lace tablecloth had done the misleading or the way that it wobbled slightly on the carpeted floor had given her the wrong impression.

It certainly didn't look like much compared to other weapons in the room. In Raven's experience, those little temporary tables in resorts were made out of PVC or something that was easy and light to transport, never convincing the user that it was actually safe to rest a beverage. But Raven now realized she wasn't at a resort and underneath the frilly lace tablecloth was the table of simplest rough wooden design. It had a square flat top that had a 12" x 12" piece of floor tile on top and was just under three feet tall, each of the four legs —a solid wood 2" x 4". In the bottom center, there was a rather large jagged piece of limestone that appeared to be glued down to add weight and keep the table from tipping over easily.

Seeing that he was repositioning to corner her further, Raven spun from behind the chair, picked up the table, and spun again using her momentum to strike the limestone end across the side of Richard's face. The little table, not built for such sport, lost its limestone decoration in the process. It released from its position to make a second impact, ironically slicing Richard's face with its jagged, glass-like edges.

Richard fell back over the tripod legs of the lighting truss hitting his head hard on the carpeted floor. Had it been a tile floor, surely it would have knocked him out, but the thick carpet had provided a cushion. While there was a lot of blood and it was a solid hit, it only resulted in knocking the wind out of him.

Seeing him having trouble breathing, Raven immediately put her right foot over his windpipe, the stiletto shoe putting just enough pressure to cut off the air supply and make him pass out. Putting her weight on the front of that foot she grabbed the camera tripod. As she was unscrewing the camera to reveal a long sharp screw at the end, she put her other stiletto on top of his privates, toes between his legs firmly on the ground, positioning the long screw under his chin. One wrong movement and the screw could be lodged in his windpipe and her stiletto would have him singing soprano.

Twenty minutes later, still standing over her captor, she felt nothing but pity. Not hatred, not anger, just sadness. The road of life with Richard could have been a much different one. She was still standing there, well . . . because she was afraid to move and was still working through a little bit of shock. Thanking the Lord, the entire time for providing her mercy, she tried to wipe away the imaginary final blow. It wouldn't take much at this point. She could rid the world of this evil and perhaps save others from this demented man. But again, she heard the words whispered from deep within, that soulful place that mattered, "What would Jesus do?" Raven was certain the answer was not killing him in cold blood. No matter what he had done, following through at this point would be murder. So, she maintained her defensive position as she collected her thoughts.

She had already begun looking around at the various cables she could use to tie him up and go for help, but whatever had been in the sip of champagne did not have her watching the road. She was not even truly sure how long they had been driving or what turns were made. Richard had been right about only three things: it was cold outside this time of year, her shoes were not designed for walking in snow and ice, and she did not have a proper coat. *One thing at a time, Raven.*

Readjusting her left stiletto to make sure it was the safety net it needed to be, she surveyed the surroundings for cables one last time. She made the plan in her mind, one step at a time. Grab that cable and tie his hands behind his back. Grab that cable and tie his feet. She had even considered wrapping cables around his entire body, imprisoning him like an inchworm, more secure and maybe even a little satisfying. Just as she began to adjust her weight, preparing to put the plan in action, she heard the frantic honking of a vehicle that was getting louder as it got closer. Then someone was pounding on the door violently. "Down here!" she called, but they couldn't hear her.

Then she heard breaking glass, the front door opening, and footsteps running down the hall. "Raven? Raven?" several familiar voices called out.

"Down here!" she yelled, "down here," the second time being a lot less of a shriek and full of thankful relief.

Multiple footsteps were heard running down the stairs towards the sound of her voice, almost all six of them reaching the door frame at the same time. They were immediately stunned and frozen in their tracks, with the exception of a small adjustment so everyone could see in. Raven, the consummate child, briefly thought they looked like the Brady Bunch all stacked up in order.

"If you could see your faces right now," said Raven as relief, disbelief, and even small smiles washed through their expression rollercoaster from the doorway, shining brightly across the ransacked room.

"Guuurl, if you could see yo'self raght now," Wally said, with his eyes wide open. On impulse, he grabbed Michael's camera and snapped a picture of her like a hunter over her prey in the amazon, not even bothering to remove it from its hanging location around Michael's neck. Of course, Raven didn't know that her full head of hair was in wild disarray, nor that she had a blackened left eye, adding to the outrageous sight before them.

Taking the first deep relaxed breath since this all started, but not budging from her position, Raven heard sirens in the distance.

"Are you going to stay there until the police arrive?" asked Fred, smiling at her as he began to make his way through the room debris. Being the shortest, Fred had had a front row seat in the doorway and now proceeded forward allowing the others passage.

Looking sheepishly at Fred, Raven admitted that she had been standing in this position so long that she wasn't sure she could move without doing some real damage on the south end of Richard's body.

"I'm kinda stuck, I think," she laughed nervously.

Still afraid that Richard was going to pop up like some scary movie as soon as she removed her foot from his wind pipe, Raven remained on guard.

Fred, unable to help himself, pretended to turn away for a moment, pointing at the left stiletto muttering the brute at least deserved that, before turning back to gently lift her up and over to a clear space on the floor. Fred might have been on the shorter side, but he made up for it in sheer strength.

By the time Raven turned around, Denny and Wally had already flipped Richard over on his stomach. Wally was standing on his hands, Denny had a foot on the small of his back and Fred was gathering cables. Raven, pointing to Michael's camera, asked him to document what they were doing so there would be no questions and also maybe to remind the men not to be overly aggressive during the hog tie. And of course, there were hugs and tears all around.

Just as the gentlemen finished securing their prisoner's restraints, chaos ensued. There were policemen running around, some taking statements from each of them, while two of the largest carried Richard upstairs hog tied and all. Angela had rushed down and straight to Raven giving her a warm hug; it was the most emotion Raven had yet to see from this new friend.

Upon seeing Angela, Denny climbed over the debris. As soon as she was free from Raven's hug, he picked up the short little woman that wielded such a powerful sword, swung her around in a loop, and kissed her on each cheek before steadying her on the ground again.

"This woman, Raven, is not to be messed with," exclaimed Denny, all the tension of the evening, as well as the relief that had been bottled up inside, expelling with his outburst. Shaking his head, chuckling to himself, he walked out the little doorway where Marna and Anna had retreated, watching the scene in awe.

Denny was so excited that when he reached Marna, he picked her up and spun her around in the same manner before kissing her full on her lips. Raven, watching both spinning scenes, quickly looked away out of respect for their privacy; however, she couldn't stop herself from thinking, for just a moment, about who looked more surprised by the action. Marna or Denny?

Moments later, Denny stuck his head back in and said, "Raven, there are some people up here who want to see you."

"You go, dear," reassured Angela. "In fact, let's gather your crew and get you out of here as fast as we can. I'll tidy up the loose ends." Grabbing her hand for a brief moment and squeezing, "I'm really glad you're all right, dear."

Then, as an afterthought as their hands dropped to their sides, she added, "I understand you host an interesting coffee talk at your place on irregular times and days. Would you be having one of those tomorrow?"

Raven, immediately catching the hint, agreed that there would most definitely be coffee talk at Bear Crossing Cabin no. 11 tomorrow morning. She was welcome to come as long as she didn't expect Raven to brush her hair, you know . . . just because she was coming! Raven made this last jest with a quick kiss on the cheek and began making her way up the stairwell.

Angela watched her exit, marveling that only the slight limp, the bruises now appearing on her arms, and the black eye getting darker by the moment, gave any indication that Raven had once again just fought for her life. A few brief moments later Angela was commanding attention.

"Ladies and gentlemen. Do you have everything you need from these fine people and may they leave?" giving the others a slight little sideways movement with her head, indicating they should head out the door.

Already upstairs was Kat, Jasmine, and Raven. When the beaten beauty first appeared, both of them started talking at once, but Raven was beginning to feel the physical exhaustion from her brawl and emotional trauma. With a quick "Sssh," she put her hands up and initiated a group hug. They stood like that for a long time, Raven leaning on them for support, finally interrupting the silence but still not moving away.

"Would you two ladies like to come have a sleepover at my house tonight?" which had the other two immediately shedding tears along with a hearty, "Yes! Yes!"

By the time everyone reached the top landing, the ladies were ready to go and they all climbed in the van. Fred was driving, with Wally in the front passenger seat. Raven, Denny, and Marna were in the first bench seat, with Denny in the middle. His right arm around Raven, on the side closest to the sliding van door, his left arm around Marna on his other side. Each lady rested their head on Denny's shoulder for most of the trip. Marna with her eyes wide open and a silly little smile that had been present since the unexpected kiss. Raven, on the other hand, drifted off to sleep, in the security of Denny's arms, within one mile of where she had been held captive.

As the trip first began, everyone sat in silence, each running through the events they had witnessed in their head. The only comment was made by Raven as she sat down hard in the front bench seat.

"I'm pressing charges this time."

While everyone could hear the comedic intent of Raven's tone, no one laughed. They didn't find it funny one little bit. Moments later, Jasmine, sitting on the last bench, squeezed in with Kat, Anna and Michael, began singing Silent Night. Her voice, soft and sincere, had everyone mesmerized for a moment, but then compelled to join in, adding harmony. Raven smiled as she dozed. She had been saying a prayer of thanks when the sounds of Heaven had reached her ears.

As they arrived at the flower shop and piled out of the van, Raven was awake, but groggy. Despite the many years that had passed between the days of sharing an apartment in college and the three of them surviving on a shoe-string budget, at that moment it was like time travel had provided them with something so familiar.

Raven had always fallen asleep on the way home from gigs and, frankly, couldn't be trusted to drive. With a giggle, Jasmine positioned herself under Raven's right arm and Kat under her left as they walked her to the waiting Beetle Bug in the parking lot. Kat had already obtained the keys from Raven's bag. Adopting her position as driver in a bit of disbelief that Raven was still driving the same old car, she tapped the dashboard as if she was greeting an old friend and pulled away as soon as all passengers were secure.

Raven was mumbling the directions and pointing. It was pretty simple. Take Main Street, northwest out of town. Turn left on the first dirt road and choose left with every option until they ended up at her doorstep. Kat and Jasmine were both remarking how they missed Raven's *sleepertainment*, as Jasmine had christened the daily event in college.

Raven didn't think she was a morning person; she mumbled and fumbled until her brain caught up with her body's wakened state and would have described herself as grumpy. However, the two girls that knew her when, and the coffee talk crew that had also experienced the phenomena, found it completely entertaining.

CHAPTER TWENTY-SEVEN

About a half hour later, the girls were laying on a padded surface they had created by throwing every blanket and rug they could find in front of the fireplace. Furniture was moved so their heads could be closer in a circle with Jasmine and Raven laying parallel to the fire, getting as close as they could. Kat got hot when she slept so she chose the perpendicular position.

Despite the group-wide agreement made as they climbed in the van to save all talking until coffee time because, of course, no one wanted to miss any of the pieces the story had to offer, the three old friends couldn't resist. The quiet conversation that ensued in front of the fireplace circled around the now historic topic, opening Raven's eyes to a piece of the puzzle she had not completely put together.

"Man, you should have seen Angela, Raven. That woman is amazing. She got in Python's face to save you. She sent the police to you and waited to make sure that Python and that actor guy that was pretending to be the band's Fan Club President were turned over properly to the police. She made us wait with her and we think we figured out why," said Jasmine.

"Wait, what? Python was involved?" asked Raven, not entirely surprised by the idea, but ignorant of the evening's events.

"We don't really know, Raven," said Kat, "we shouldn't be speculating. All we know is what we saw, not really what it means."

"Okay, so what did you see?" asked Raven, curiosity overwhelming her, needing all the answers to truly end the ongoing nightmare.

Jasmine, unable to help herself, was still so excited to have Raven back that she didn't give Kat a chance. Kat didn't mind. Their relationship worked that way.

"Well," started Jasmine, "Angela said something about a file on her desk, and suspected Python was involved. She got right in her face, which eventually led to her handing over the address where you were, but it was when the police got there that was really interesting."

Jasmine continued breathlessly like she was talking about a surprise movie ending not yet revealed. "Angela pulled a file out of her briefcase that looked like she had been carrying it around for a while. It was all tattered and worn. All she said was she wanted to assist in pressing charges for both events and everything they needed to start connecting the dots was in the file."

At first, this comment had Raven's thoughts twisting and turning in all directions, but the roads didn't take her far. She was exhausted and somewhere around the idea that Python might have orchestrated the whole thing, her thought-mobile halted. Closing her eyes, she fell into a dreamless, hard sleep, thankful that none of them had chosen to bring Richard into the conversation.

CHAPTER TWENTY-EIGHT

Raven awoke the next morning, sore from head to toe and her left eye and cheek were feeling extremely tender. Kat was snoring slightly and Jasmine was balled into the fetal position with the covers almost completely covering her from head to toe.

The sun was creeping in through the glass exit to the patio overlooking the lake. Raven never closed the drapes. She preferred to see the beautiful canvas nature presented every time she walked into the room. Right now, she was thankful the drapes were open for a different reason. As the sun shone down on her body, it was as if an instant healing power was at work. The warmth that covered her was a synergistic example of how nature fit together.

For a moment Raven fantasized she was related to Superman. How could she possibly pass up that movie reference? But as she moved to stand she recognized that, alas, she was a mere mortal as every muscle in her body began to scream again.

Sneaking down the hall quietly, she made a quick stop in the restroom before heading to the doorway at the end of the hall. Raven hadn't shown this room to the girls last night and, hearing the piano calling to her, she began to play and sing the first Christmas carol that she could think of, Joy to the World. By the middle of the first song, the girls had followed the sounds to the end of the hallway at Bear Crossing Cabin no. 11 and stood in the doorway, aghast and elated.

Kat looked relaxed and cool, like she had just jumped out of a van full of hippies, stress-free and just a bit sloppy.

Jasmine. on the other hand. looked like she always did in the morning, her hair sticking straight up and out . . . and the true birthright for the endearing name, *Jasmania.*

When Wally and Fred arrived, the girls were jamming freestyle, just remembering what it was like to live inside the music bubble together as a team. After a loud round of applause, Wally announced that Fred was cooking, which had the three ladies immediately standing up and heading to the kitchen. They were starving.

"Happy Christmas Eve!" Fred exclaimed as the rowdy group came bursting into the kitchen, everyone responding in the same manner as Raven sat down in her favorite chair, with the ladies grabbing seats around the table. Wally began counting on his fingers and then moved to the living room where the distinct sound of furniture being shuffled drifted to their ears from the distance. Shortly after, she could hear Denny and Marna in the living room with Wally. They must have come in the front entrance, Raven mused, chuckling to herself as she realized she had never even opened that door.

Just at that moment Anna and Michael, followed by Angela, strolled in with additional Christmas Eve greetings. Then, to Raven's surprise, Dreyfus stood in the doorway with a strange goofy grin plastered on his face. With a dramatic jump to the side and comical "Tada!", he revealed that Jessie was hiding behind him.

"Jessie!" jumped Raven, running over to hug her friend and the others as they entered the room.

"Dreyfus, what a nice surprise," said Raven

"Denny called me last night and filled me in. He asked me to pick up Jessie here and bring her in time for the party, so here we are! Glad you are okay," he said sincerely, obviously happy to be included.

"And I jumped on the red eye to come see your black eye!" exclaimed Jessie as she inspected her friend's injuries, a slight grimace indicating her underlying emotion of the second attack.

Raven hugged her friend again, assuring Jessie she was indeed unharmed, followed by a little happy dance. Was it possible that all of her favorite people in the world were gathered in this one little room, or did she actually not win the battle the previous evening and this is what Heaven looked like. Shaking the tears of joy from her head, she followed everyone into the living room. Fred was leading with a tray of eggs. Dreyfus, taking the hint, grabbed the bacon while Michael brought up the rear of the food chain with the blueberry pancakes.

As they drifted into the room where the fire had been restocked, most of the blankets that had been on the floor were now balled up in a corner. Others were draped over the easy chairs and sofa. Denny was returning from the kitchen with chairs under his arms. After everyone was seated, with Jessie and Raven taking their standard favorite place on the floor in front of the fire, she noticed the tree.

Standing to the right of the fireplace was a Christmas tree surrounded by boxes of lovely decorations on the floor. Raven had never had a "real" Christmas tree as Denny well knew. Sean and Lydia would have surely replaced their manufactured version for a real one if they could've seen the current childlike wonder of excitement and happiness on Raven's face.

Denny explained to Raven, of course, that this particular tree had not been murdered unnecessarily for their entertainment, that the tree had to be cleared for the project, and had nominated itself for this particular purpose.

He added this point, smiling at the precious memory where she had confided her desire to decorate a real Christmas tree. She had looked up at him pointedly, not more than eight years of age and said, "But in the ground of course. No need to kill it for a few days of dress-up."

CHAPTER TWENTY-NINE

The talk over breakfast was non-consequential, mostly everyone sharing humorous stories of Christmases past. But once their bellies were full, the lights had been hung on the tree, and they were all sitting down to a nice cup of coffee, silence fell. Wally finally put a spotlight on the big elephant in the room by stating with an official, booming news anchor voice.

"And now, ladies and gentlemen, it is time for the wrap-up soap opera saga, *As the Raven Flies*," which had Angela and Fred falling out of their chairs with laughter.

Raven couldn't help but join in. It was easy to laugh now that it was over. The questions. The fear. The blame. The hiding. The feelings of betrayal. They were all gone and all Raven could think about was the joy found in that very moment.

No one was quite sure where to start; it was Denny that suggested Angela take the floor. He recognized that she, out of all of them, could get past the subject quickly and efficiently. Angela agreed, for she had been fighting the urge to make a suggestion all morning and perhaps this would be her chance.

"Raven," Angela smiled sincerely, Raven noticing the dark circles under Angela's eyes for the first time, making her wonder if Angela had slept at all the night before. "I'm afraid there is more to this story than you are aware. All of you," Angela said, sighing behind her kind eyes as she looked around, notably stopping with direct eye contact at Kat, Jasmine, and Denny.

"First, there have been three arrests," she continued, choosing her words carefully, desiring to relay the twin stories together succinctly.

"Three?" said Raven in surprise, others echoing the sentiment.

"Yes, three: Richard, Argus, and Python. It pains me to tell you that Python was the mastermind behind the first plan, sending you off on your own solo, using Richard and Argus as her pawns in the plot. In the simplest of terms, Argus and Python were aware that Richard was still alive and he was blackmailing them this second time. Apparently, he could connect the dots on that terrible place in Connecticut that burned down, as well as the forged paperwork indicating Raven's agreement with the solo plan."

This announcement had both Kat and Jasmine gasping and swearing under their breath, but Angela didn't give them the opportunity to dwell.

"Now, I don't presume to know if Python understood he would go as far as he did in Connecticut, but she knew where you were the entire time you were held captive. Obviously, she has been terminated from Diamond Back Records and I have agreed to testify in court."

"How did you find out about all of this?" Raven blurted out, not as flabbergasted as everyone else in the room. Raven had already come to that conclusion herself the night before. While she had ignored the nagging feeling that had been running around her brain since that time, Angela's words were just confirmation that Python was ultimately responsible for putting Raven in that position.

"Your file, Raven. You see, I had Argus escorted out of the building almost the minute I took charge. I had worked with him in the past and had no tolerance for his means or methods. Much later I found myself in the position of needing his office. We had been so busy that we had just been grabbing what we needed out of his file system, as we needed it; and frankly, his office had just been used as a storage space for years. However, once we started looking at everything and scrubbing his computer, we found some things that were more interesting, like cryptic emails and copies of your signature. Argus was definitely a shady character, but apparently not a criminal mastermind.

"Once we connected some of the documentation, and I had your file in my hands, I discovered the letters you wrote to the CEO concerning Richard. Something didn't feel right. So, I dug deeper," she explained.

"This required some doing and quite a bit of time, but we now have some amazing IT techs on staff. They are the ones that siphoned through the network backups. Richard was much more careful, but in the end, I had deduced there was a third party that had set Project Solo Raven in play. I just didn't have proof. I also couldn't connect any of that to your physical trauma. When I met you, you seemed content to leave everything behind, so I put the file in my briefcase and have carried it with me ever since. I'm fairly certain that we have enough proof now.

"So, Raven, Jasmine and Kat, you were all played. No matter how the situation might have been handled better, or the varying differences of suffering, you were all duped. I'm glad you are no longer letting that stand in the way of friendship. I've seen the music business rip apart more relationships than I care to admit," Angela shook her head, her voice now trailing off, her story complete.

Once again, Denny marveled at how Angela was able to use just the right amount of words to describe the decade of events, leaving no questions in his mind and wasting no time.

Angela, remembering the nagging suggestion that had been jabbing her brain, continued a moment more, "Raven, there was no way to stop the news reports. There were just too many people aware of the happenings. Some fans were even posting "Original Raven Missing" before we had even determined you truly were. So of course, there are all kinds of stories running. If you are up to it, I suggest you do a press release as quickly as possible to get it all out in the open so you can truly move on. Just a suggestion, of course, dear," Angela smiled sincerely.

Recognizing immediately that the woman before her was not making the suggestion for selfish means, Raven agreed to think about it. Truthfully, though, had no idea what she would say.

The next couple of hours had them decorating the tree and enjoying each other's company, ending with everyone out in the back yard by the lake making snow angels and snowmen as beautiful ornate flakes began to fly in the wind. The morning's festivities ended with a huge snowball fight that had Raven and Wally fighting against everyone else . . . and winning.

Around 1:00 the impromptu Christmas party guests disbanded to prepare for the evening festivities. After the previous evening's events, Denny had decided to close the bar for the early shift, only opening for the Christmas Eve gathering and musical event.

Kat, Jasmine, and Angela were all sent to Cabin no. 7, one of the larger cabins that actually had separate bedrooms. Dreyfus went to Denny's; and Jessie, recognizing Raven needed some time alone to process all that had happened told Raven she was going to Denny's to hang out too, to call her if she wanted company.

Raven hugged her dear friend tight, expressing her excitement that she was there. With a quick kiss on the cheek, the trio was walking up towards Cabin no. 1, following Wally's and Fred's snow footprints most of the way.

CHAPTER THIRTY

Alone with her thoughts for the first time since the ordeal began, Raven pondered Angela's suggestion.

All this time Raven had been thinking that putting the story into words allowed the darkness to persist, but that was her doing with or without the words. Perhaps her story could bring hope or strength to others that found themselves in abusive situations. Perhaps her speaking the words and not hiding the truth would actually empower her, and others, forging ahead as a victim of circumstance; but, not allowing the victimized persona to engulf them, become them.

Without any clear answers, Raven did what she always did. She turned off the water in the sink, left the remaining dishes for later, and retreated to the comfort and solitude of prayer at the piano bench.

CHAPTER THIRTY-ONE

When Raven arrived at Denny's Den at two minutes to 4:00 p.m., just like she always did for any scheduled shift, you could taste the excitement in the air. The bar was packed, much to Raven's surprise. It was not anything like the cozy gathering she had previously imagined and desired. Of course, the entire small population of Jackson Hole had heard about the events of the evening before and had seemingly decided to all join the little Bear Crossing's family for Christmas Eve.

Raven, with a guitar strapped on her back, had to squeeze through the crowd as people shouted "hello" and "so glad you're alright." Of course, there were whispers too, especially after she turned and waved to the crowd of friends, her black eye shining through the curtain of curls like a laser beacon . . . but so did her smile.

The evening turned out to be one that Jackson Hole would talk about for a long time. The *Mashed* band was not scheduled; its members were home celebrating the holiday with their families. Kevin, Randy, and Seth had actually landed their first official group gig at a Christmas party on the other side of town. They had even invited Bernie, the now infamous *Jugman*, to join them.

Raven, knowing this ahead of time and quite happy for her comrades, had brought her guitar . . . for Denny. If everything was to come full circle, it had to start at the beginning.

So, the first half hour, until Denny cried uncle claiming his fingers were out of shape and needed callouses, Denny and Raven played through all of their old favorites, only this time she played the piano. Every once in a while, you could hear additional angelic harmony as Kat and Jasmine joined in from the audience. It was just beautiful enough to catch your attention and just light enough to make you wonder if it was even really there.

Later in the evening, Kat and Jasmine joined her on stage and, to Raven's surprise, Elizabeth Tonkem had arrived and offered to play guitar. Raven welcomed Elizabeth to the stage warmly. Glancing at her former band mates, she could see they were happy with this invitation.

"Elizabeth is cool, Raven," Jasmine had shared around the fire the night before with Kat nodding in agreement. "She never liked or paid attention to all the Ravyn stuff and was always careful to not claim any responsibility for your work. She just wanted to play music. In some ways, she reminded us of you. You will like her if you ever meet!"

Jasmine and Kat were correct. Five minutes into knowing her on stage, without yet having a conversation, Raven already liked her. Not only was she a true musical-team player, but you could sense the vibe of her personality through her guitar prowess.

At the end of the first couple of songs, Jasmine and Kat were exclaiming their surprise at Elizabeth's guitar skills, which only had the girl laughing and admitting, "I would have rather played guitar all along!" The girls, knowing that Python never would have allowed that, understood why the newest bandmate had never crossed that bridge.

Angela, of course, was beside herself. Seeing the four women on stage and enjoying the family atmosphere was far more than she had hoped for; and, if you were sitting close enough, you might have heard her shake her head into her martini saying, "Faith is a funny thing, Lord. I know I waivered there for a minute. But it worked out just like you said it would. God bless us all."

Angela had always been a servant of the Lord. Her footsteps sometimes faltered when the voice inside spoke to her; but, she had never swerved in her devotion, not even when her young daughter was killed stepping into the middle of a domestic battle. She had lost her best friend of many years and her beautiful daughter that night when her friend's ex-husband had climbed

244

through the window, intent on having the last word on her leaving him. Helping to save Raven from a similar abuse, and bringing these girls back together served as a healing bandage, in some small magical way.

Angela's thoughts were interrupted as Wally announced his newest ARTbender special, the *Christmas Kiss*, an announcement that had everyone running to the bar to sample the secret recipe. Raven assumed it would have a hint of Peppermint Schnapps, a fact that was confirmed as Angela brought her a sample before patting her shoulder at the piano and returning to her seat.

During this set transformation, Raven had simply begun playing Christmas carols as background filler. Jessie and Dreyfus, who were sitting right up front, began singing to the music, quite loudly with glee. Raven couldn't help but laugh at her old friend, who made up the words as she went along. She had never been good with lyrics. It was obvious that Dreyfus found this completely amusing and endearing as he tried to help her out with over- zealous articulation. It wasn't long before others followed suit, joining in the musical comradery. The volume made Raven scan the room again. She was surprised by the number of happy faces looking back at her. Not only did it appear that no one had left, but in fact, many more people had joined them.

Raven had a sneaking suspicion that Michael had streamed the impromptu *Kissed* jam session, enticing additional locals and visiting tourists to travel and join in the fun. As the volume of audience Christmas karaoke began to subside Raven launched into a beautiful, mesmerizing rendition of Away in the Manger, during which she caught Angela's eyes again. Angela, recognizing the need for encouragement, responded with an understanding nod, a kind-hearted smile and confident gaze. It was time. Raven agreed.

Scanning for Michael, their eyes connected and Raven motioned for him to roll tape. Jumping in gear, Michael was nodding and giving a thumbs-up almost immediately. *The boy was fast!*

"On behalf of all of us at Denny's Den, Merry Christmas everyone," Raven shared over the microphone, "I want to thank you all for being here tonight. For your well wishes and support too. Sincerely, thank you from the bottom of my heart. I am quite happy to have made my *permanent home* right here in Jackson Hole, surrounded by all of you amazing people," an announcement that elicited spontaneous cheers around the room.

"Over the last few months you have been introduced to my hidden past. A truthful, yet lacking many details, story about how my life changed so many years ago. As a good friend recently stated, it's time to set the story straight."

Raven continued to play the piano softly in the background, mentally sifting through the details, searching for the words that would set her free.

"Nine years ago, I was taken hostage for three months by a man I trusted and called my best friend for many years. During that long window of time I was abused in every form possible: mentally, emotionally, physically, verbally, and sexually. While we thought that man had perished in a fire, that was not the case."

Everyone in the room who had been reading the blog knew the only fire mentioned had Richard's name connected, the savior that took them from shoestring to stardom. Even over the piano, Raven could hear the gasps and whispers pass as the information processed.

"Last night, I was again taken hostage by the same man that had no desire other than to own me like a piece of property. I look pretty bad, I know, but *this time,* he looks worse. I am happy to say that the man and his accomplices are now behind bars.

"Many of you are curious about what happened to me. That's natural. I had told myself I was hiding and covering up the truth to protect you; but, of course that is not the *whole* truth. I believe tonight, we will *all* get the answers we want and need.

"Before I share the rest of my story, let me interject that I am happy to have the *Kissed* family back in my life, including the newest member; and, while I will not be going on tour would welcome any project they put before me here in Jackson Hole," she said with a winking hint to the three girls standing in front of Wally at the bar.

"Second, if the Bear Crossing Board accepts the presentation, which how could they not when I'm sharing it in front of all of you, Bear Crossing will be adding a facility to train women, and men, in self-defense. There will also be housing for those that have suffered abuse and have no other options."

Denny interjected with an "All those in favor, say Aye!"

"Aye" resounded loudly from the entire crowd, not just the board.

"Since moving here, you've heard me say several times that I am more comfortable sharing my feelings through music. If you will allow me to play three songs for you, I think your curiosity will be quelled; and, God willing, I will be able to leave this darkness where it belongs, in the past. It is going to take a slight dark turn, but if you stick with me to the end, you will join me in the beautiful peaceful place where I now sit.

"I won't take you through all the stages of fear and grief, but when I was at the very bottom, wondering if I could continue, this song is what pulled me through to the other side."

ALL I NEED

I can't believe that I'm again sitting here.
Feeling so alone, when I know You are so near.
Lately I find there's an emptiness within.
Maybe it'd be easier if I'd just give in.

But then again, every lesson must be learned,
And when I stray, You guide my safe return.
Just when I think, there's no more I can bear,
I turn to You, You are always there.

So, I will stand strong,
No matter what may come.
I won't be down for long,
Now the battle has begun.
My faith will win, I'll never give in,
Because it's true, it's You.
You're all I need.

Sometimes it seems like the world's closing in on me.
No peace to be found, chaos at my feet.
But with a single prayer, You dry my tears.
And with a gentle Hand, You vanquish my fears.

So, I can stand strong,
No matter what may come.
I won't be down for long,
Yes, the battle has begun.
My faith will win, I'll never give in,
Because it's true, it's You,
You are all I need.

And when it seems every hour is getting worse,
And every word I speak feels like it's a curse,
I turn to You to set my spirit free.
Yes, I turn to You, because I believe.

That I can stand strong,
No matter what may come.
I won't be down for long,
Soon the battle will be won.
My faith will win, I'll never give in.
Because it's true, it's You,
You are all I need.

It's true, it's You,
You are all I need.

After a short pause, letting the last note on the piano ring into silence, Raven introduced the next song,

"And of course, there was the anger, which Jessie and Denny suffered through daily. You will now be forced to suffer through it for approximately three minutes and forty seconds," an aside that had the crowd chuckling through teary eyes.

PRISON OF REGRET

You don't see it,
How you push me,
How you try to take control.

Your obsession,
With a connection,
Is like a toxin for my soul.

You're a user,
An abuser,
A reflection you can't see.

When I don't bow down,
To your desires,
You point your mirror only at me.

And I never wanted anything
But peace and love for you.
And I never asked you for anything,
And you hate that you know that's true.

Do what you want, I have no shame.
I'm not gonna fall, my soul won't stray.
This prison of regret is all you're gonna get.
And maybe one day you will see,
How your love poisoned me.

You try to change me,
Manipulate me,
So you can feel more like a man.

Your words and actions,
They are so crazy,
A twisted version of romance.

But you don't own me,
Don't even know me,
So, stop right there in your tracks.

You can't convince me,
Bend or break me,
Your love's a sharp knife in my back.

And I never wanted anything but
Peace and love for you.
And I never asked you for anything,
And you hate that you know that's true.

Do what you want, I have no shame.
I'm not gonna fall, my soul won't stray.
This prison of regret is all you're gonna get.
And maybe one day you will see,
How your love poisoned me.

This prison of regret is all you're gonna get,
And maybe one day you will see
How your love poisoned me.

Mesmerized by the emotional performance you could hear nothing but crickets in the room, the audience lost in the space Raven had just created.

"And that leads us to the final number, before we all retreat to our homes to celebrate the glorious anniversary of our Savior's birth."

Taking her fingers off the piano, her hands suddenly shaking, she pulled the hair tie off her wrist. A motion that exposed many green and purple bruises in the process. This was it, the unveiling. The moment of closure where she could truly move on and focus on the life and gifts He had provided to her.

She was nervous because in the last nine years she had come to terms with the facial destruction, but the apparent motivation still haunted her. And while the brief glimpse captured by the initial video had provided the proof that all was not right, it didn't tell the whole story.

Tears glistening in his eyes with much emotion and some pride, Denny watched his Goddaughter face her fears. With visibly trembling hands Raven pulled back her hair carefully and completely, making Denny understand why Raven had returned the piano to the "wrong side" of the stage, as she had called it.

Again, Raven could hear the expected gasps as people viewed the sight of her face that no plastic surgeon had been able to repair. Denny's tears fell full force at this time, unable to stop the pain he felt for the girl he loved so dearly. Across the damaged cheekbone and scarred skin, you could clearly see one word that until today had desperately haunted her.

That one word, surrounded by many other scars lighter in color, stood out jaggedly upon her face as if it had been carved using an old rusty wood-burning kit, the poorly repaired skin sinking into the etchings, forever more; the damage could not be repaired.

Putting her hands back on the piano as everyone in the room stared with tears in their eyes, some turning away, trying not to imagine how that word had ended up there. It wasn't small either. It began just under her left cheekbone and extended back to just below her ear.

Taking a deep breath, she said softly into the microphone, "We don't always understand the journey or the challenges we face that bring us home to this place of peace, love and harmony; but, this horrifying saga led me here."

Her focused waivered slightly as she heard sobbing around the room, those closest to her and some she hardly knew, fighting to hold in the empathetic pain.

"Dry your tears, my dear family and friends. For it is not a time of sadness. Today is a time to rejoice. I am finally home in more ways than one. This raven sits alone in the darkness, *nevermore*."

You say I'm yours, I say I'm His.
In his image is the only way that I wish to live.
You say I'm yours, I say I'm His.
And with every breath I breathe,
I'll give all that I can give.

You can brand me, break me, burn me, stake me,
Fool me, cheat me, use me, beat me,
I'm still free. I still believe.

You say I'm yours, I say I'm His.
In his image is the only way that I wish to live.
You say I'm yours, I say I'm His.
And with every breath I breathe,
I'll give all that I can give.

And your selfish claims, your words are all in vain.
You can't see. Obsessed with your own need.
And you carved your mark like you owned my heart,
But I'm still free. I still believe.

You say I'm yours, I say I'm His.
In his image is the way that I wish to live.
You say I'm yours, I say I'm His.

You say I'm yours, I say I'm His.

ALMOST TWO

YEARS LATER

ALMOST TWO YEARS LATER

Coffee talk at Cabin no. 11 was on the patio this fine Sunday morning. Everyone was eating breakfast BBQ pizza from Mario's and watching the winter dance antics of Raven's little feathered raven friend, who had become a frequent visitor. Although they had seen him enough that the bird no longer paid them any attention, they continued to enjoy each show like it was their first. Raven was a little bit awestruck too, but for different reasons. She was looking around the crew's new favorite spot to meet, everyone in place. The fire pit was blazing, its red-hot coals warming just enough for comfort in their coats and scarves.

Denny and Marna, now married and expecting their first child, were on her right in a wooden loveseat rocker built for two. Denny's left arm was around his wife's shoulders and the other one was resting on her belly, his face beaming with joy. Raven and Fred had already been honored with the title of Godparents. Raven had excitedly and quickly transformed the smaller guestroom space into a nursery, counting the days.

Marna had closed her flower shop on the edge of town and now managed the little Bear Crossing Gift Shop. It had some flowers, but Marna had really turned it into something special for their little community by adding branded keepsakes. Her very friendly and competent assistant, Cheryl, did most of the legwork now. Marna was finishing things up in her clothing studio, preparing to take maternity leave.

Her first inspirations, no surprise, were for toddlers. She had created a whole line of baby clothes, waiting for her precious one to arrive. They were only offered on order at this point, but Angela had dropped a hint that a friend of hers just happened to be a buyer for one of the top clothing distributors and would be visiting her soon . . . soon meaning whenever Marna was ready. Of course, the baby would change everything so no decisions were being made at this point.

Fred was in the chair next to Denny with his feet up on the edge of the fire pit, completely relaxed. Wally was next in line, sitting on a stool that was way too small for him; crouching over further to get as close to the raven as he could get without insulting the bird, watching it intently, completely entertained. Fred, of course, was watching Wally, also completely entertained.

Fred had gotten his new kitchen and was even writing a cookbook, each recipe to be paired with a delicious recommendation by Wally the ARTbender. Wally was getting very little sleep these days, but it didn't slow him down any. The construction of his brand-new theater was almost finished and he was already beginning to set up a show schedule. Everyone in town had promised to audition and Wally had promised that everyone who wanted to be involved could be involved, as long as he was the lead, of course. "Well, at least some of the time," he would smile and clarify sheepishly. Truthfully, the entire town was buzzing. The quality of the upcoming theater might be questionable, but there would be no lack of fun and family festivities.

Next in the circle was Dreyfus and then Jessie, both sitting in the loveseat rocker's twin. Construction of Dreyfus's cabin/office had been completed quickly and he was spending more and more time in Bear Crossing. While Raven was thrilled at how easy that made everything, she knew he wasn't here for her. Unbeknownst to Raven, Jessie and Dreyfus had hit it off upon their first meeting and six months ago Jessie was standing at Raven's door with a suitcase yelling "Surprise, I'm relocating to Jackson Hole!"

In her hand, she had an ad for employment and her sincere question, "Do you need a résumé?" had Raven laughing outright at the woman who brought her back from nothing.

Jessie was now living in her spare room and managing the self-defense clinic, along with the related housing. Raven loved having Jessie here and made the most of every minute because she knew it wouldn't last. It wouldn't be long until Jessie was moving over to the other side of the property. There were definitely wedding bells for the two of them in the future.

Diamond Back Records had rented a cabin for year-round use. You never knew who you might find playing down at Denny's Den with Raven on a given weekend. More often than not, however, you saw Angela, who had become one of the family. Angela was at the moment sitting on Raven's left in a single wooden rocker, a fleece blanket held up to her nose with pure contentment and joy in her eyes, still holding a half-eaten piece of breakfast pizza in her right hand.

Michael was sitting on another stool to Angela's left, looking much more comfortable than Wally. The young man was excelling in school and his blog had made him famous. He had many interviews under his belt, along with footage no one else would ever get because no other cameras were ever allowed inside of Denny's except his. This single rule allowed musicians to come to Bear Crossing to relax away from the prying eyes of the media, and yet still get great coverage for any music they produced.

Raven had noticed that Angela was bringing in more and more artists that never toured, never allowed any cameras, thus giving Michael yet another opportunity to excel. Despite the attention and amazing opportunity, Michael was unchanged. He was still the same goofy kid Raven had met years ago, only now he had more hair on his face.

Raven herself had been busy. She was teaching many different types of classes. She still worked at the bar as much as she could, even though she was never officially on the schedule anymore. She performed at Denny's regularly and, as promised, with Angela's help, she released that first album the day they broke ground.

The album was a collection of heartfelt recovery songs intended to be inspiration for victims of abuse, but as today's time is filled with so much despair (and perhaps because of the extra press received about the motivation behind the album), sales sky-rocketed. It was a feat that ensured not only the building of the self-defense clinic and housing, but also secured staff members and the cushion that Bear Crossing needed in order for the plan to work at all.

The big surprise for Raven had been Angela's suggestion for the album cover artwork. "It's brilliant," she had said through streaming tears after hearing the collection of songs for the first time, obviously touched by the listening experience. Angela then paused before reaching into her briefcase, finally deciding to pull out the photograph that had lived there for a while and place it face down on the table.

Meeting Raven's gaze she said, "Just think about it," as she flipped over the picture revealing a close-up of Raven's freshly destroyed face. "I pulled this from the file I gave the police officers that night they carted off Python. I figured if during all that time you hadn't shared the extent of your scars with others, I wasn't going to let someone leak it to the press for a free cruise! Now, however, maybe it's time you share it yourself."

While a bit gruesome, it was also perfect, and did indeed relinquish Raven's remaining burden. Despite her unveiling that Christmas Eve, there were still feelings that sometimes made her want to hide from it herself. Releasing it on the album cover and mentally redefining the carver's hand to be His hand—the hand that saved her and protected her, the hand that loved and guided her—was the last step needed to truly let go.

Her journey may have been tough, but she would not be the person she was today without that bumpy ride. And whatever bumpy roads lay ahead, she would face them head on with faith, knowing that she was His, and that on the other side she would find peace once again . . . and of course, another lesson learned.

Thank you, Lord. Life is good.

They sat there around the fire pit at Bear Crossing Cabin no. 11 for a long time, admiring the beauty before them and simply enjoying the serenity of the morning.

"You know, I've been thinking," said Raven, breaking the comfortable silence with a very serious tone as little tiny ornate flakes flurried across her face.

"I've been here almost three years now, and I have never seen a bear."

The Dawn of Eve

Chronicles of Eve Wilder Book I

A novel by:
Yvonne DeBandi

Eve Wilder was on a mission to discover what killed more than 99% of the population. So many had died and so fast...

"Horrible, vivid visions flooded my memory as I cut the brush away to clear our path. With each machete strike I could see another terrified lifeless face, another fire, another mass grave site...until finally, Jack and I seemed to be the last ones left. It took a few days to manage the shock but we eventually packed our bags, boarded a motorcycle and got out of town. I had no idea where we were going to go, but one thing was certain...we weren't staying there."

Eve, a former professional musician, has been told she is the key to their survival. She journeys across the Rocky Mountains slowly unraveling a conspiracy of surprising magnitude, an unbelievable rabbit hole designed and orchestrated by a few people in power. Unfortunately, something went wrong and now the world is dying.

Join Eve and the team of warriors she meets along the way as they discover the truth. Will they be able to save the human race and heal the earth?

Made in the USA
Columbia, SC
25 January 2023

10184891R00146